Angelborn

JK Allen

*To my sister, Carol, for always being on my side and my biggest fan.
And to Sherry, for being a dear friend and a big help in so many ways.*

Prologue

Aiden turned the page silently in the halo of his flashlight. It was late and he'd be in big trouble if his parents knew he was still awake. But he had to know what happened next. Things were just getting exciting, and soon they'd figure out who the baddie was. All he needed was one more chapter.

The house was peaceful. Everyone was asleep except him. He loved the freedom he felt in these quiet moments. Where it was just him with his thoughts. He could imagine himself as anything. A great warrior or a magician. He loved the twins, his little sisters, but they were always vying for his time and attention. He was never alone except at bed time, and he relished this time. He grabbed the juice box off the stand next to his bed and took a sip, turning another page.

He paused, juice mid-air. Had he heard a noise? His heart beat faster and he swallowed hard. He put the juice down and dropped his book, ears straining. His parents were all the way down at the end of the hallway. He knew he should wake them, but that meant walking past the stairs. If someone was down there, they would definitely see him.

A cold sweat broke out on his neck. There was another noise, closer this time. Then he heard it. Maniacal laughter.

"Kill them all." The voice was low and cold. Aiden shivered.

Squeals answered the dark voice, then there was the

noise of some kind of animal tearing its way up the stairs. Aiden sat bolt upright, his heart pounding in his ears. Down the hall, a door crashed open.

"What on Earth?" his dad cried out. His mother yelped, then screamed. A loud clatter traveled down the hall. It sounded like a fight. Both of them screamed together. Aiden was frozen in bed. Helpless.

He heard claws scrambling across the floor, then the door next to his room was flung open. The girls. They shrieked and called for help. Aiden could only imagine what they were seeing, what could scrape across the floor like that. The footfalls were heavy, the claws long and clacking hard, tearing into the floor with each step. The girls' cries rose higher and higher. Aiden clawed at his ears, desperate for the sounds to stop. Their voices held so much pain and fear. He couldn't take it. He pulled the sheet up over his head, rocking back and forth without noticing.

A loud thump filled the room and the screams all stopped. He could smell his sweat trapped under the sheet. Everything was silent. Awful, agonizing silence with only his breath to keep him company. Were they all dead? That was the only thing that silence could mean. They were gone. And he had done nothing to help them.

The tears came then. He stifled a sob, praying desperately they wouldn't hear him or find him. For surely he was next. He thought about hiding, but he couldn't move. All he could do was sit there under the stuffy sheet and wait for death. He squeezed his eyes shut tight, the tears streaming down his face. There were the claws dragging on the floor in the girls' room.

Turning—whatever it was—it was turning. Soon it would be in the hall, then at the door, then. He couldn't finish the thought. Hot tears slipped out, and he gripped the sheet in his hands until his knuckles turned white. He couldn't breathe. He yanked the sheet off his head, taking a big gulp of air. It was time now. Time to die.

Then the silence shattered. The front door burst open and the sound of boots pounded through the house and up the stairs. Inhuman shrieks filled the air, and then faded. His door knob turned, and Aiden held his breath. He wasn't ready.

The door opened. An Asian man stood in the frame,

haloed by the light from the hall.

"You are safe now, Aiden." His voice was so full of confidence, Aiden almost believed him. But then he looked down and saw the monster at his feet. Three inch long black claws covered in blood and sharp fanged teeth protruded from a creature that resembled a grotesque, oversized weasel. This must have been the monster that he heard. It's claws that ran into his sisters' room and made those terrible sounds. But it was dead now at this man's feet. Had the man killed it? Did he kill it in time?

"Did you save them?" Aiden's voice was small and high pitched. "I couldn't move. I couldn't help them."

"I'm sorry, Aiden. It is not your fault though. It is not your fault at all." He walked towards Aiden slowly, hands up where he could see them. He sat at the foot of the bed. "My name is Jackson." He held out his hand.

Aiden took it clumsily, most adults didn't shake hands with kids. "I'm Aiden."

"Yes, I know. I am going to take you somewhere safe now. Is that alright?"

Aiden couldn't think. He wasn't supposed to go with strangers. But this man had known his name and had killed the monster. He struggled with what to do, his mind tumultuous.

"My dad says I'm not supposed to go with strangers," he managed to get out. He watched his hands, still clutching the clammy sheet. Tears fell at the thought of his father. He would never see him again, never hear his voice.

"You are right, but I am not a stranger. I knew your mom. That's how I knew your name was Aiden. You see, I am part of an organization that helps people."

"You mean when the monsters come?"

"Precisely. We stop the monsters when they are hurting people. Now I just want to get you somewhere safe in case more monsters come."

Aiden's eyes went wide and he started trembling. *Were more of those things on the way?* He shuddered at the thought.

"You are safe with me, Aiden," Jackson reassured him, placing a soothing hand on his arm. "But it is best if we leave right now. Is that okay?"

"I still can't move," Aiden said through tears, his

voice breaking.

"It is okay. I will carry you. You do not have to move."

Jackson gently pulled the sheet from Aiden's grip and scooped him up into his arms. Aiden breathed in his scent, and it calmed him, just like it did being in his dad's arms. His hands relaxed and he took in a few shaky breaths.

"Just keep breathing, Aiden," Jackson said, rubbing his back. Aiden was still crying. He tried to stop, but the tears kept coming. "It is okay to cry," Jackson reassured him in soothing tones.

Jackson buckled him into a car outside the house. Aiden watched as his house got smaller in the back window. He wondered if he would ever see it again. He cried harder at the thought. He knew he'd never see his family again. They were gone forever, and it was all his fault. If only he had woken Dad up when he first heard the noise. They were all dead because of him. He was the one that should have died, not them. What was he going to do now?

They pulled up to a huge mansion. He'd never seen a house this big before.

"Where are we?"

"It is called Alliance House. Shall we go inside?"

Aiden nodded, but didn't move. Jackson came round to his side and opened the door. He even leaned in to unbuckle him. Then, after a slight pause, he lifted Aiden out of the car and into his arms. Aiden linked his arms behind Jackson's neck.

"How old are you, Aiden?"

"Ten."

"You are getting big."

"I'm sorry."

Jackson shook his head. "There is nothing for you to be sorry about. It is no problem for me to carry you. I do not mind at all."

"I could have woke my dad up. I heard a noise." Aiden

sniffed as he felt more hot tears coming as they walked into the house. He felt the need to confess to Jackson, the enormity of his sins.

Jackson paused in the foyer. "If you had, you might not be alive. Have you thought of that? You did what you could to stay alive."

"My dad could have fought the monster."

He pushed his glasses up his nose and looked hard at Aiden. "There was more than one, Aiden. And they are not easy to fight. Your father did not have the weapons he needed to fight them. It is not your fault."

Aiden looked down. "I could have done something. But I didn't. I was scared."

"Everyone gets scared. It is nothing to feel ashamed of. Do you like reading?"

Aiden nodded, wiping away tears.

"Look at this room then."

Jackson opened a heavy wooden door to a huge library. The walls were completely filled with books, except for where a large fireplace stood. Extra bookshelves filled the space in the room. It would take decades to finish reading all these books.

"Wow, that's a lot of books." Aiden couldn't hide his astonishment, giving Jackson a watery smile.

"Would you like to pick one out to read?" Jackson asked. When Aiden nodded, he walked to the back wall, which held books for younger readers, and set him down. "Pick any book you would like."

Aiden looked around for a long while before selecting a book with pirates on the cover. He walked up to Jackson, holding it out to him.

"Ah, one for adventure, I see." Jackson smiled at him, and Aiden shyly returned it. "Let us go somewhere cozier, shall we? What is your favorite color?"

"Blue, I guess."

"Blue it is, then."

Jackson took Aiden by the hand and led him out of the room. His mind was whirling like a tornado. He had no idea what he was meant to do or feel other than to follow this stranger around an even stranger house on the strangest, most horrific night of his life.

They climbed some stairs, then turned down a hall

until they reached a blue bedroom. It was even close to the shade of blue his room at home was. *Home.* It tore at his heart to even think the word.

Jackson walked him inside the room, closing the door. There was a bed, desk, and dresser in the simple room. Jackson pulled back the covers on the bed, then placed Aiden in the bed, tucking him in. "You relax, and I will read the book to you."

He sat down at the chair in front of the desk and, clearing his throat, he began. It had been years since Aiden had been read to like that. His parents had loved him—he knew this without a doubt—but with the twins, it was hard to find time for Aiden and things like reading together. Aiden had always missed the bedtime stories, though he had never complained about not having them anymore. Now, Aiden was getting his wish to be read to again, but he would much rather have his family.

Still, Jackson's voice was pleasant and soothing. Aiden settled back into the bed, adjusting the pillow under his head. Before he knew it, he was lost in the story. Aiden soaked in the words. The sound of Jackson's voice filling his head, quieting his racing mind. Aiden closed his eyes, tonight was a night for darkness, after all. A night when you've lost everything. His breathing slowed. The words were a steady stream and, drop by drop, the story poured into him until he was so heavy with words that he slept.

When Aiden woke late the next morning, he had a moment of calm. A moment where he felt more at peace than he ever had. The last wisps of his dream were floating out of his head as he sat up. But then he stopped, staring hard at the unfamiliar room.

It was stark, containing nothing that marked it as someone's room. And it most certainly wasn't Aiden's room. Then, like a vise on his chest, the night before came flooding back into his memory. The harsh voice, the monsters, the screams of his family, then the silence and Jackson opening the door.

His family was gone. Just like that, he was alone in the world. Everything had changed, and he struggled to catch his breath. Grief descended upon him, a hungry vulture set on cleaning the bones of his soul clean. His grief opened up like a vast expanse, until it was bigger than his little body could contain. Tears seeped from his eyes, and a strangled cry caught in his throat. What would happen to him now?

His palms grew clammy as he clutched at the sheet. Sweat formed on his brow. Who would want him? This boy who had sat by silent as his family was killed. This boy too afraid to save the ones he supposedly loved more than life. He hung his head in shame, tears dripping from the tip of his nose. He was worse than useless. And now, he was alone.

But this couldn't have been the first time this had happened. Jackson said he worked for people who fought the monsters, who protected people from them. A hope flared up like a rocket in Aiden, a hope that he could help others. Stop the tragedy that had happened to him from destroying another family. That he could learn to fight these monsters, to kill them, to keep others safe. He seized upon the idea with the ferocity of a passionate ten-year-old. This is what he wanted to do with the rest of his life. This was how he would atone. This would make his loss mean more than just death.

He wiped his tears away with an impatient arm and got out of bed. He would find Jackson, and he would start his new life saving others now.

Chapter 1

The night looked frozen in time as Jacob made his way to his newly rebuilt lake house. A hot wind rustled through the trees, ruffling his dark hair. The lake house was the proverbial phoenix, rising out of the ashes of the fire that had killed most of Jacob's family. But he did not mourn them as he approached the house. Tonight marked a new beginning for Jacob, and Lake Locke reflected the jagged shards of stars as they twinkled in the deep night. The lake was smooth; not even a ripple marred its surface, and it made this moment infinite, drawing out before him. Jacob fingered the signet ring he always wore, checked his phone for the time, and hurried his steps forward.

Jacob entered the house, feeling the cool metal of the handle under his hand; and the chill in the air reminded him of a tomb. Smiling, he descended into his favorite room of the renovated home, the dungeon. Chains studded the wall along with knives, picks, clamps, and mallets. They dangled from the ceiling and crowded a long table. Planks ran eye-level across the far wall, parallel to the ones that ran along the baseboard. A disheveled old man was tied to one, his head and large paunch hung down in defeat.

"Welcome to my lair," Jacob spoke quietly. "You know where we are, don't you?" He couldn't help but smile as he ran his fingers across the instruments of torture on the table next to him.

"You." The old man's watery blue eyes widened, and he squirmed against the wall.

"Me. Of course you know who I am. My family owned this house long ago. I've made improvements, as you can see." Jacob gestured to the room. "You are the Secret Keeper, and you have kept my secret. Perhaps I should thank you. It's thanks to you that my plans will succeed." Jacob savored each word and the look of hatred on the old man's face. He loved this game and reveled in the role he played.

"Son of serpents, go back to your place in perdition," the old man spat before succumbing to a coughing spell.

"You'll see perdition long before I will, old man. But, before you do," he paused and picked up a long metal spike that narrowed to a needle-thin point. "I have a few questions."

"You can't do this!" The Keeper's eyes widened again, and he pushed back against the planks as though that kept him safely out of reach. Jacob smiled, knowing he had the leisure to enjoy breaking this scum and knowing he would soon have the final key for his plans. There was much to celebrate and much to enjoy. The Keeper would give him both.

He twirled the spike in his hands, then turned his attention to his guest. "I already have. You're here, aren't you?"

"You won't get away with this. The Alliance...."

"Is too weak to stop me. After all, they've forbidden my very existence and yet," Jacob spread his arms wide, "here I am. And better still, they don't know I am here. Once again, thanks to you."

The old man rasped, his chest heaving heavily under his own battered weight, "Grace will stop you."

Jacob's handsome face turned into a grimace at the mere sound of the name. Then he picked up a mallet off the table, a complement to the spike in his other hand. He grabbed the Keeper's hand, squeezed his flesh until it was a nice shade of rosy pink, and then slammed it against the plank. Jacob placed the spike against the old man's pinkie and drove the mallet home. The screams were wasted in the soundproof room, but Jacob savored each one. Spike after spike found its way into the Keeper's sagging flesh.

"Give me the name of the child," Jacob stated, each word drawn out.

Tears trickled down the Keeper's face, but he looked up at the mention of a child. Surprise and horror were etched on his face.

"Oh yes, I know he has recently fathered a child. Give me the name or...." Jacob let his eyes wander to the Keeper's hand, finger after finger pinned to the wall, held still by a combination of steel spikes and Jacob's malice.

A pause as the Keeper realized the awful truth. "No..." the Keeper muttered. Sweat trickled down his face. Jacob could smell his fear thick in the air.

He smiled, almost letting forth a chuckle as he walked to the table. Brandishing a curved knife, he returned to the Keeper. No longer content to play games, he rested the tip just below the old man's left eye. "The name," he repeated.

"Gracehurst," the Keeper gasped.

Jacob dug the knife tip in and watched drops of blood well up and trickle down the old man's cheek. "The full name."

"Evangeline," he muttered, "Lise Gracehurst."

Jacob smiled and drew back the knife. "Well now, that wasn't so difficult was it?" His eyes glinted.

"God forgive me," the old man mumbled as he closed his eyes. His thin lips moved in prayer.

Jacob's hand snaked out, the tip of the knife leading as he plunged the blade deep into the Keeper's throat. With a quick slash, he ripped the blade from one end to the other. The Keeper slumped, his shoulders folded unnaturally. He had served his purpose well, so Jacob granted him a swift death. He dropped the knife on the table with a hollow thud. Grabbing a towel to wipe the blood from his hands, he walked away from the smell of acrid sweat and copper and out of the room. He whistled, savoring the thrill of the moment, the moment he had heard her name. The moment his real life would begin.

"Take our guest home," Jacob said to Mordecai.

Mordecai bowed and smiled wide. "My lord," he replied curtly then disappeared into the dungeon.

"Marta," Jacob acknowledged the woman standing at the top of the stairs.

Her black and white hair was pulled back into a severe

bun that made her hooked nose even more prominent.

"You have learned the name, yes?"

"I have," Jacob replied almost nonchalantly.

As he passed her, Jacob couldn't help but notice a wicked smile on her lips and a fierce hunger in her eyes. "Good," she said, stroking his cheek. "Your plan is working."

Chapter 2

It always started with maniacal laughter. Then a dark voice boomed, "Kill them all." Aiden heard the screams of his family in hot flashes, each another stone in his stomach. His sisters' were the worst. The twins were just seven years old. They shrieked, and Aiden clawed at his ears to block out the sound as he sat there, unable to move, waiting for death as he sat in the shadows that swathed his room.

He awoke with a start, grabbing the key and ring that always hung about his neck with trembling hands. Tangled in his sheets, his shirt stuck to his back, he shivered as he took in big gulps of air. Aiden waited for his dream to fade, for his memories to return to ghosts once more, then yanked his shirt off. Swallowing past the lump in his throat, he rubbed his eyes until the afterimages of the dream were wiped away. It had been seven long years, and yet it felt like it was yesterday when he had lost them. Would he never be free of that pain? Seven years had transformed him from a child into a man. He could only hold out hope that these nightmares would end in time. He got up and stripped the sheets off the bed.

Aiden remembered everything about that night when he had first arrived at the Alliance House. He had awoken to chaos, the screams of his family and the discordant scratches of claws on wood. His sisters' voices had risen higher and higher until a loud thump silenced them. It was such a horrible, solid sound. Awful, agonizing silence caused a hush to fall throughout the house. There was only the sound of his heartbeat and the smell of sweat as he cowered under his blanket.

Then the silence shattered. Footsteps, heavy and surefooted, pounded below and echoed up the stairs. Inhuman shrieks filled the air then faded. His door opened and a man stood haloed in the light that cascaded in from the hall; a hideous monster at his feet. Aiden wondered if angels actually had halos. He would find out soon enough.

That was the moment Jackson had come into his life. Jackson had read to Aiden that first night at the Alliance House; the first time anyone had in years. Aiden soaked in the words until he was saturated with the color and sound of each one, emphasized by the sound and cadence of Jackson's voice. Drop by drop, the story poured into him until he was so heavy with words that he slept. The next day Aiden had been heavy with guilt instead. The ache that opened inside him at the thought of his family seemed a bigger gulf than his body. It surpassed his flesh. It would devour him until he was nothing, like a black hole. Still, he had begged Jackson to join the Alliance in order to keep others safe from the terror he had somehow survived. At ten years old, he had chosen the path of the Alliance.

He splashed cold water on his face and studied his reflection. Dark circles were prevalent underneath wide open eyes and his skin was pale in the grey light of dawn. His reflection looked haunted. How many times had he relived the horror of that night? Aiden had lost count. With a sigh, Aiden stepped into the shower. He let the water cascade down his face and body, relishing in the feel of the hot water for a few minutes before turning the tap towards cold. When he was done, he dressed methodically in the first shirt and jeans he grabbed, they were mostly all the same colors anyway, then remade his bed and headed downstairs.

He ran into Jackson sitting alone at the kitchen table. Soft yellow sunlight was beginning to filter down from the high windows.

"You are up early." Jackson looked up from his cup of coffee, probably his second of the morning. He saw the bundled sheets in Aiden's hands. "Bad dreams again?"

"It's not a big deal."

He raised a brow above his glasses before continuing. "You should take care of that, and then meet me in the library."

Aiden nodded.

"The danishes are good this morning," Jackson said. A subtle reminder for Aiden to eat something.

A few minutes later found Aiden sitting across from Jackson's oversized desk with a danish in his hand. Jackson took off his glasses and wiped them on his shirt, a faraway look in his eyes. His face seemed more lined than it had been yesterday and his salt-and-pepper hair was more mussed than Jackson ever let it get. Aiden watched the flames crackle in the fireplace.

"There has been a lot of activity lately. Changelings," Jackson said, sitting up and replacing his glasses.

"There's always some around."

"This is different; our sensors indicate a greater demon may be in town."

"Greater demons can't stay in this realm."

"It is hard to say exactly what the situation is. Still, our sensors are not wrong. They have been showing previously-unheard-of levels."

Jackson slid a manila folder across the desk towards Aiden. A picture of a man not much older than himself fell out. He had black hair, grey eyes, and a smile that twisted upwards into a devious snarl.

"That is Jacob Kingsley. He seems to be the changeling in charge of this little group. They are responsible for crimes ranging from petty theft to drug dealing. However, they have graduated to the big leagues. We have reason to believe Jacob and his crew are responsible for the murder of our Secret Keeper."

Aiden snapped straight up in his seat, mouth open as his mind raced with the consequences of those words. "The Secret Keeper?"

"We found him yesterday. They tortured him. Probably for information. Which information, however, is unclear at this point. Something was taken from his apartment, something important. We need to know what Jacob is up to, and who he is working for."

Aiden let Jackson's words sink in, his stomach leaden and churning. No wonder Jackson's face was lined and looked strained. One of the Burned Ones had tortured a Keeper for information. The whole notion was dangerous for the Alliance.

Jackson readjusted his glasses. "I want you to shadow Jacob. You must not be seen. You are not to discuss this matter with anyone else. Report to me directly. Promise me. Absolute secrecy is required for this mission, do you understand me?"

"Yes."

"Then promise." Jackson's look bored into Aiden as he swallowed past the lump in his throat.

"I promise," Aiden said, standing tall. He grabbed the file and returned to his room to go over it and craft his plans. He would get to the bottom of this, he had to.

Chapter 3

Ginny hopped onto a nearby picnic table with a groan as she watched Pat disappear into the crowds. They were bored. It was yet another Friday night at the carnival that set up shop in downtown Lockewood every summer. Pat insisted on one too many turns on the Tilt-A-Whirl and had left to grab drinks while Ginny recovered. The night held a mugginess to it. The kind of night where the air felt thick and soupy as it settled against her skin. But a breeze blew in from the river, bringing some relief. Ginny propped herself up with her hands behind her and looked up at the stars. The breeze made it easier to breathe, but she could still feel the weight of the crowds surrounding her.

Her eyes were still skyward when someone fell bodily into her, knocking her clear off the table. She twisted painfully and then fell, landing on her now-throbbing knee and bruised elbow. The guy who had landed on her scampered off before Ginny could stand up or see her assailant.

Of course this would happen. Of course she would get clotheslined by some random boy here in front of everyone. Her cheeks burned and her palms grew sweaty as she looked around.

"Hey! Where do you think you are going?" Pat called after the disappearing group of boys. He'd returned just in time to see the tackle, and the two drinks in Pat's hands were being shaken to death as he screamed after them. Ginny's face grew even hotter. Now Pat was drawing even more attention, the idiot.

"Put down those drinks before you spill any more on yourself," Ginny said as she sat up and looked her knee over.

"Are you okay?" Pat asked, a hint of sympathy in his voice.

Ginny's knee throbbed and felt strained. A livid welt the size of her thumb had left its angry red mark on her knee. She sucked air in through her teeth as she touched it. Her other leg was mostly unscathed, other than a small scrape on her shin. She stood up, cheeks still hot, and brushed herself off.

"I think I may die of shame."

"I only caught the last part as they were running off. What happened anyway?" Pat asked, picking up one of the sodas and taking a long drink.

"You were there, you tell me," Ginny said, hands on hips.

"Wish I could," Pat said, setting down the drinks and running his hand through his hair. "You didn't see anything?"

"Like I was paying attention. I wasn't expecting to be assaulted at the fair."

"Fair enough." Pat chuckled as Ginny shot him an exasperated sigh. "Those guys were drunk and rough-housing, and one of the guys launched the dude that hit you right at you. Not cool that they just took off like that."

"Well, an apology would have been nice, but it wouldn't fix my knee. Just forget it."

"If I had been there...."

Ginny rolled her eyes. "You'd have worse bruises than me."

A boy her age walked towards them, and Ginny stopped in her tracks. Tall and lithe, he moved with a dancer's grace as he drew nearer. Next to his tousled black hair, his blue eyes were a striking contrast. Ginny shook her head to clear it, heart skipping a beat as their eyes met. He grinned at her and she swallowed hard, wondering why this handsome stranger had stopped serendipitously in front of her.

"Are you okay?" he asked, a soft look on his face.

"Umm...." Her mind buzzed as she stared at him, mouth agape. Suddenly she found herself speechless.

"Did you know that guy?" he asked.

"I didn't even see him. Otherwise I would've, you know, gotten out of the way and not been trampled."

He laughed, and it transformed his face into something soft and genuine. Ginny's heart beat faster.

"Um," Pat's brown eyes regarded her strangely, "who are you exactly?"

"I'm Aiden," he offered her his hand.

She took it, acutely aware of how warm it was as it engulfed hers.

"Ginny."

"Beautiful name for a beautiful girl. I'm very pleased to meet you."

"What do you want?" Pat interrupted, crossing his arms. "Are you with those clowns or something?"

"No. I would never join those scum," he said as a gust of wind blew his bangs to the side. His voice was low as he watched the direction they had taken off in. "I'll be on my way now," Aiden said, turning to face Ginny. "I hope we meet again." And with that, he turned and left in the direction those boys had run.

"What a joke. 'Beautiful name for a beautiful girl,'" Pat mocked in a higher pitch. "So cheesy." He scowled at Aiden's retreating figure.

"What's your problem?"

"Oh don't tell me that worked on you, and you fell for that crap?" Ginny's eyes narrowed, but he continued on despite the warning. "You're not stupid, gin and tonic."

Ginny turned to glare at her best friend. "Oh, so I'm stupid for not hating a complete stranger who's done absolutely nothing wrong?"

"That's not what I meant... you know that."

Ginny stalked off in the opposite direction. "I'm going home." Her voice was somber from the searing pain in her knee that radiated throughout her body with each jarring step she took. The walk home would be torture, but there was nothing to do but to face it.

Pat rushed to get in front of her. "Know what you used to love and adore?"

"What?"

"Piggyback rides. My mom thought you'd throw my back out."

"I was seven."

"Feel like reliving the past?" Pat waggled his eyebrows like Groucho Marx, and Ginny couldn't help but laugh. She wouldn't make it the whole walk home without help either.

"I'm only agreeing for the sheer joy of it and not because I'm incapacitated."

"But of course," Pat said with a bow before he crouched in front of her.

A gentle wind rustled the trees as Ginny and Pat wandered beneath them, the leaves sleepy as they fluttered to the lullaby of the breeze. Despite the street lights, Ginny could make out the twinkling constellations of stars as they shifted overhead. Pat strode down the familiar streets of their neighborhood and regaled her with tales of his step-brother, Cody. Pat and Cody were a week apart in age and got along well. When Pat wasn't with Ginny, he could be found with Cody, along with Andy and Josh, their best friends.

"Hey PJs," Ginny interrupted with her nickname for Patrick Jorden. "When will you have your driver's license?"

"Before summer's over. Noah promised to take us for the test before school starts up. Maybe a week or two."

"Are you going to fight Cody for the car keys every week?"

"Nah, that guy will most likely fail the first time, and then ask this guy for rides all the time. I bet I can make him do all my chores when he really needs a ride somewhere."

"I am not doing you any favors just to get a ride."

"Of course you won't, hence why I must make him do it. And, here we are." He gently let her down in front of her porch.

Ginny hobbled up the steps to her porch. She paused and glanced back at Pat, who wore a strange look on his face. "Do you want to come in?"

"No, I'm working for Noah early in the morning. Ice your knee and stay off it." His step-dad was a carpenter and Pat worked with him every summer.

She rolled her eyes. "It's just a bruise."

"Ice it anyway."

"Yes, mom. Now scram and get some sleep. You're working with dangerous machinery tomorrow."

"Sweet dreams, gin and tonic."

"Sweet dreams, PJs."

Pat rolled his eyes as he headed down the road. Ginny watched him for a moment, his true height hidden by his slouched figure, his shaggy blonde hair falling disheveled in every direction.

The sharp pain in her knee brought her back to herself and she limped inside. There was only the flickering light and muted sounds of the television in her mom's room. Asleep as usual. Ginny shuffled past her mom's room to her own. She heaved a sigh of relief and collapsed onto the bed.

Her room, in true style, was covered in different colors as her favorite colors had evolved throughout her life, from a layer of pink to green to purple. The only constants were the photos she had framed; one of her mom, one hazy pic of her dad, one of Pat, and one of Pat's whole family. Tonight she was drawn to the picture of her dad. Like all her memories of him, the picture was out of focus, just a brilliant smile under a big floppy hat, and Ginny in his arms laughing. She wished she could hear her father's laughter now. She wished she remembered what it felt like to talk with him. But all she had was a blurry photo and some other keepsakes. A tear, warm against her cheek, escaped the corners of her eyes as she lay back in bed, the picture held close to her chest. What could she even remember of him? He had died when she was three. A vibrant smile and the trust of being held close was the most she could summon. She tried to recall the scent of his arms around her or the sound of his loving voice, but couldn't. An ache opened up inside her chest. More tears slipped out, and she closed her eyes to block out everything. She rolled to her side, the picture crooked under her hand as she fell asleep, exhausted.

Ginny stood before a door covered in an ornate

pattern of carved flames. She hesitated, not sure if she should knock. The door opened without so much as a touch, and she peered inside, curiosity getting the best of her. Cloaked in shadows, the room was spacious. The only light came from a large hearth where a multi-colored flame blazed with shifting colors, beautiful enough to mesmerize anyone for hours. Golden baubles of every shape and size adorned the walls save for one. The far wall was covered with an intricate family tree written in a language Ginny had never seen before. The room was warm and smelled lightly sweet, like incense burned at Christmas. The warm, fragrant air surrounded her, cloaking her in comfort.

She walked towards the fire and watched the colors of the rainbow bend and shimmer, and didn't notice the man who had walked in.

"The fire purifies," a familiar voice said behind her.

Ginny turned to see a man wearing a low hood, hiding most of his face. But he smiled at her, and she felt a warmth surge through her, washing any fears away.

"Welcome, my child." His voice echoed off the high ceiling.

She moved to step towards him, but the pain in her knee stopped her short, just feet from the grate.

"You're hurt?" The surprise in his voice was disconcerting.

"Oh, I hurt my knee tonight." She took another step towards the colored flames. "It's just a bruise really."

"Please sit," he gestured to the love chair next to the fire. "I'm afraid it's not a bruise. You've been marked."

Whatever that means. She sat and blew her hair out of her face.

"You are in danger, I'm afraid."

Ginny laughed. "That's impossible. I'm just a teenager."

He looked at her sadly. "You must beware of the snake in the grass. Not all who smile are friends. But, not all is lost, there are those who would help you." The fire crackled and leapt high into the air.

"More snakes?"

"Yes and no. They are your sworn brothers. They can protect you."

"Who?" She raised her head and gave him a piercing

look. "Who?"

He raised his hand to brush the hair from her eyes, but stopped himself, his hand dropping to his lap as he smiled at her sadly. "I can't lift the mark in this ethereal realm, but I can ease the pain." He placed his hand on her knee and with a touch as light as feathers, he wiped her pain away with the soft brush of his hand. She sighed, and he smiled at her. It was such a beautiful and warm smile that the tension and worry built up inside her melted away in its wake.

"You need rest now. Be brave and be strong. Everything changes now. Sleep, my child."

His hand brushed her brow, and she fell backwards into darkness

Chapter 4

Aiden had watched Jacob and his men for days now, and he was surprised to see large groups of changelings—the humans who drank demon blood for its powers at the cost of their humanity and souls—mingling with the humans who worked for Jacob. He was still waiting for a hint of what had happened to the Secret Keeper. Aiden strolled through the Alliance house, the big, rambling mansion he'd called home the last seven years, his thoughts weighing heavily on his mind. He needed food and sleep and was just making his way towards the kitchen at the center of the house when Tali ambushed him, again.

Stopping just in front of him, his best friend stomped her foot down and her hands flew to her hips. "Where on earth have you been?" she asked, narrowing her dark brown eyes. Tali closely resembled her father with her brown skin, dark eyes, and sly smile she usually wore, but that was where the similarities ended. Her disposition was as far from their laidback healer as you could get, and now he was facing her wrath.

Aiden ran his fingers through his hair and stared at the ceiling in a vain attempt to avoid eye contact. "Tali, you know I can't tell you that."

"That's absurd. We're friends, right?"

"I have strict orders."

"He couldn't have been doing anything that important." Ari wore a haughty look as he strode towards them. "After all, no one would trust him with anything important."

Aiden clenched his jaw. "Funny you mention that, because someone did," he said through gritted teeth.

"You're just pretending you can't talk about it so we won't laugh at what you've really been doing."

"And you're just jealous they gave this mission to me and not you."

"That's a laugh," Ari said, stepping in front of Aiden. "As if I'd ever be jealous of a nobody like you. You aren't even angelborn." Ari turned his back to Aiden, his head jutted into the air in arrogance. His very smile was painted in disdain across his features.

Aiden's face went hot. He wanted more than anything to knock Ari down a peg or two, but he had no comeback for that remark. He wasn't angelborn. He couldn't combat the truth. Yet here was Ari, nearly dripping in superiority and disdain, and Aiden could do nothing to set things right.

"He may not be angelborn, but at least he's a decent person. You don't qualify," Tali said while crossing her arms.

"What do you know about it anyway?" Ari said, waving his hand. "My point still stands."

"You don't have a point," Tali said.

He spun to face both of them again. "My point is I'm angelborn, my father is a Council leader. I'm way better than Aiden in every way. Nothing could ever make me jealous of you," he turned and looked Aiden square in the eye. "You're just an orphan, a nobody in a sea of nobodies."

Aiden seethed, fist clenched, he anchored his shoulder back ready to strike.

"Aiden King," Jackson shouted down the hall. "Report to the library at once."

Ari snickered as Jackson rounded on him. "Wipe that smirk of your face, Ari, and go to your room. I do not want to see you until morning."

"I'm not a child," Ari said, his voice high. "You can't just send me to my room."

"Is that the case?" Jackson strode towards them with quick steps. "Shall we call your father and tell him why you have to be treated like a child?" he asked, staring Ari down.

"No," Ari said quietly, ears red.

"Room, now." Jackson pointed up the stairs.

Ari threw Aiden one last nasty look before he took the stairs two at a time.

"Aiden, do not make me repeat myself."

Aiden turned on his heel and walked to the library. What a mess tonight was. But it never hurt to see Ari reprimanded for being an ass. His footsteps were muffled by the thick rug that ran along the hallway up to the ornate mahogany doors of the library. Just before he reached the door he heard Jackson talking to Tali in low tones.

"You know he is not allowed to talk about what he is doing, so why do you insist he tell you? Do you think your judgment is better than mine? Or perhaps do you think you are above the rules all members must follow?"

"No," Tali squeaked. Aiden caught a glimpse of her face flushing as he shut the door.

"You certainly know how to cause problems," Jackson said as he entered. "But Tali should leave you alone for a few days."

Aiden nodded, still fuming from Ari's harsh words.

"You need to control your temper better," Jackson said as if reading Aiden's mind. "Even when he deserves it, you cannot start a physical altercation with him. Imagine what his father would do. You have to be the bigger person. Do you understand?" He sat down with a groan in the plush chair behind his oversized desk. The desk was always kept tidy besides the stack of papers to one side and the piles of books on the other.

"Yes," Aiden said, heaving a sigh. "I know exactly what his father would do." Aiden looked around at the cases of books that filled the room. A large portrait of a famous leader hung over the fireplace, looking down at them menacingly.

"You would be out of the Alliance permanently. He has been looking for a reason to expel you; do not give him one."

He's right of course. Aiden had to admit it to himself. "I'll control my temper."

Jackson looked into Aiden's eyes for a moment before he nodded and glanced down at his papers.

"What do you have to report today?"

"Nothing new, yet. Jacob's been away from the warehouse and it's business as usual for his gang of criminals. There's been some mention of a book I couldn't understand." Aiden leaned back in his seat, the portrait of the council leader grimacing at him.

"A book?" Jackson looked up, peering at him over his glasses.

"They call it *the* book, pretty important apparently. The changelings seem happy Jacob has it, though the humans have no knowledge of it."

"Anything else about the book?" Jackson stared at him intently.

"No, but they've also talked about a house on the lake. I think that's where Jacob stays."

He raised a brow. "Anything specific about the lake house?"

"It's large. Three or four stories. There's always a guard patrol at the house. They had to clean it out a week ago."

"The Secret Keeper," Jackson said in a whisper.

"You mean...?" Aiden's mind whirled.

"We have our own clean-up crews, Aiden."

"They get rid of the bodies of changelings and demons, so people don't notice them."

"And Jacob had a body of his own to dispose of last week. The Keeper was found in his residence after he had gone missing for a few days." He rubbed his forehead and winced.

"This means Jacob did kill the Keeper." Aiden's voice had gone soft as he met Jackson's gaze.

"It affirms my suspicions at least. We need to find out why Jacob killed him. We need to know his plans."

"I'll get to the bottom of this."

"Get some sleep. You look exhausted," Jackson said, rubbing his neck.

Aiden nodded and left the room. He no longer had any appetite, so he headed up the stairs straight to his room. Aiden ignored the portraits and oil paintings that lined the walls, staring at the thick, patterned rug beneath his feet instead. Opening his door revealed a meticulously clean room, dotted with pictures of his family on his dresser and the full bookcase next to his desk. The room was blue, his favorite color since he'd first arrived there. It was the same shade as his old room, the last remnant of his old life that had given him a sense of familiarity all those years ago. Now, he couldn't be bothered with things like favorite colors. Closing the door behind him, he stripped out of his clothes, turned off the light, and climbed into bed. He fell asleep as soon as he closed his eyes.

Chapter 5

Ginny woke up in pain. Her knee throbbed and she felt the edge of irritability running through her. She looked at her knee and groaned. The thumb-shaped welt was red and swollen. In fact, her whole knee was swollen. Wasn't this supposed to get better? She ran a hand down her face and reached for her phone.

"Gin and tonic," Pat's reassuring voice filled her ear.

She huffed out air. "I need a best friend day."

"Gladly, but is everything alright?"

"Yeah," she said with a sigh. "I just woke up on the wrong side of the bed."

"Well, we'll get you right in no time." She could hear the smile in his voice and grinned. "Let's grab brunch at Lucky's."

"Sounds good. Just have to get ready."

"See you soon."

Ginny hung up, feeling much better. A day with Pat was just what she needed. Of course he didn't need to know her knee was getting worse. He would just worry. It was the same reason she hadn't mentioned it to her mom. She felt bad enough, she didn't need them hovering over her as well.

She took a shower and got ready as fast as she could hobble about, then texted Pat she was on the way. The walk to Lucky's wasn't easy. A jolt of pain lanced up her leg with every step, but she tried to enjoy the feeling of the sun's warmth on her shoulders as the birds sang around her.

Pat was already in their usual spot when she arrived, and she gave him a big smile as she joined him.

"You don't seem too grouchy," he said, taking a gulp of his soda and pushing the hair out of his eyes.

"Gee, thanks." She grabbed a menu even though she had it memorized.

"Ah, there it is."

She stuck out her tongue, and he gave her a playful smile.

"How's your knee?"

"Better," she lied through her teeth, forcing a grin.

"Well, it must still be a little sore."

"Oh, a bit. But I'm kind of used to it now."

"You're weird. You would get used to pain." He laughed as the waitress approached.

They ordered and made small talk about Pat's summer job with Noah. His latest project was his most difficult one yet.

"It's really intricate woodwork." Pat shook his head. "It's almost beyond me."

"You're an artist. I bet you're great at it."

He shook his head emphatically. "Noah's the expert, not me."

She put back the menu and looked at him squarely. "But you've been helping him for a while. Don't discredit yourself completely."

He sighed, but smiled finally. "Well, I can say it's going to look awesome when it's all said and done."

Pat had a steadier hand than Cody, Noah's son. Not to mention an artist's eye and the patience required for the job. He'd helped him for some years now outside of school hours. Cody worked at the local grocery store instead. He enjoyed the small talk that came with the job.

Their food came, Ginny got strawberry pancakes and sausage, and they got to work, chowing down. When they were done, they both sat back and smiled.

"So what else is on the agenda for today?" Pat asked, rubbing his stomach.

"We could always have a bad movie marathon."

He nodded. "And I got new oil pastels. We could

always experiment with those too.”

“I’m game,” Ginny said, digging in her purse for money to pay the bill.

They cashed out and walked to Pat’s house. She did her best not to limp or grimace as they weaved through their neighborhood. Kids ran after an ice cream truck, shrieking with joy.

“Hey, weirdos,” Cody said as they walked in the door. He had a triple decker sandwich in his hand, his brown hair curling around his ears. He smiled at them, his green eyes crinkling at the corners.

“You’re one to talk,” Pat replied dryly.

“Great comeback.” Cody rolled his eyes. “How’s it going, Gin?”

“Just fine. How are you?”

“Saving up for a new game. It’s a first-person shooter, and it’s supposed to be epic.”

“Sounds cool.” Ginny could only nod and smile. She was not a gamer. Not that she had anything against it, she just never knew how to play properly. She was a dreaded button masher.

“Eh, it’s something to do,” Cody said with a shrug. “What are you two up to?”

“I got new art supplies. We were going to check them out,” Pat said, rubbing his hands together.

“You spend all your money on art supplies. No wonder you don’t have a life.”

Pat rolled his eyes. “Says the guy saving up for a video game.”

They both laughed. Teasing each other was how they bonded. They were actually very close, even if they didn’t always seem like it.

Ginny loved working with the oil pastels. The smooth glide of pigment on paper and the vibrant pigments were enough to win her over. Of course, her attempts at a sea landscape were clumsy compared to Pat’s masterpieces. But she was used to that by now. Pat always eclipsed her in art, always had.

“These are so cool,” she said, holding up her drawing for Pat to see.

“Yeah, I don’t know why I’ve never tried them before. I love how they blend.” He gave her a thumbs up. Blending, she knew she had forgotten something. She laughed as she set aside her seascape.

After drawing, they watched some bad movies in the game room in the basement. Cody had gone out with Andy and Josh, so the TV was free. Pat's mom, Jane, popped in to invite Ginny to dinner. She happily agreed. Jane made the best dinners. Ginny wasn't much of a cook herself, and her mom was usually working, so a real dinner was a treat she didn't turn down often.

"So what's new with you, Ginny dear?" Jane asked, placing dishes on the table. She had her blonde hair coiffed in an elegant bun, unlike her son's unruly hair. She also had blue eyes instead of brown, but Pat shared the same upturned nose as her.

"Let me help," Ginny said, grabbing a plate of asparagus.

"Thanks, dear." Jane smiled at her, showing off perfect teeth.

"Nothing new really. Just enjoying my summer," Ginny answered as she grabbed another plate of food.

"Well, it's nice to have you over. I'm still used to seeing you every day. We miss you when you aren't around."

Ginny had spent her days after school with Pat while her mother worked. She blushed, but smiled. "Thanks, it's nice to be here. Especially for dinner. You're an amazing cook."

They were all seated and had served themselves when Noah walked in. He looked tired but happy as he joined them.

"Where's the squirt?" he asked of Cody. A nickname Cody loathed of course, and Pat would never let him live down.

"Hanging out with Andy and Josh," Pat answered, grabbing more potatoes.

Noah nodded. "Going to need you this weekend. If Ginny can spare you, that is." He laughed, but Ginny flushed, putting down her fork.

Sure they were best friends, but Ginny didn't like what Noah was implying. She most certainly didn't own Pat or any of his time. He could do whatever he wanted. It's not like they were dating. It was especially not like they were dating.

"Noah," Jane scolded. "Ginny doesn't monopolize his time."

"I didn't mean she did," Noah said, clearing his throat and noticing her flushed face. He took a drink of water, a little red in the face himself.

"I can work this weekend," Pat said quietly, not looking up as he stabbed a spear of asparagus.

Ginny left after dinner, feeling exhausted. She climbed into bed and grabbed her journal. Her mind felt tangled and she tried to write down her feelings to figure them out. She wrote about her knee hurting, the strange dream she'd had and the hooded man's warning, and what Noah had said at dinner. She rankled at the comment still. Pat didn't need her permission to do anything. They were just friends. They'd been friends for forever. That would never change. Surely no one expected anything else, did they?

Her brow furrowed as she contemplated that question. It didn't matter what other people thought of course. She knew the truth, and Pat knew the truth. Didn't they?

The rest of her evening was uneventful. She caught up on her favorite show and went to bed early. But try as she might, she was more upset by Noah's comment than she wanted to admit to. She fell asleep still thinking about it.

Chapter 6

Kitty-corner from Jacob's headquarters in an abandoned building, Aiden watched the gang from his vantage point on the second floor. Aiden crouched low, getting into position. The sheer number of changelings all in one room was previously unheard of, but everything about Jacob was confusing and unexpected. It was strange so many changelings would be gathered together without their demon master there to keep them in line. And why was Jacob the changeling in charge of all the others? Where was the greater demon the sensor kept tracking?

Aiden shook his head and pulled off one of the two necklaces he wore on his person at all times. This one was his scribe. The scribe looked a little like the cigarette holders women used in the 1920s, only not as long and tipped with what looked like golden chalk. They were made from aoiveae, a glowing silver blessed metal, and seraphite, which was a golden chalk-like substance the Alliance used to write the Angelic Script.

Strictly speaking, Aiden wasn't an Alliance member, not where it counted anyway. He had spent the last seven years living, eating, breathing, fighting, studying, and doing all things Alliance, but he wasn't a blood descendant of the angel. This meant that he could use the scribe to write sigils that did work, just not as strongly as it worked for the angelborn. Concentrating on nothing but the sigil he had to write, Aiden crouched with his scribe ready. The sigil he needed would allow him to see and hear from a distance, and he worked silently as he wrote it. The seraphite flashed gold before seeping into his upturned palm.

With a gust of wind, his ears suddenly registered new sounds: a bird pecking at the road below, shifting drafts of air in the old building, and the occupants across the street that he could now see with an eerie clarity. He could even see the sweat that rolled off one changeling's neck as he glanced nervously at another scowling changeling.

"I told you to watch her until you were relieved. What are you doing back?" the nervous one demanded. His dark hair was matted to his forehead.

"You're not in a position to tell me anything." Arrogance seemed to roll off of this one.

"This is too important for you to mess up."

"You go watch her paint if it's so important."

"I will not tolerate your insolence," the nervous one said, but his voice cracked.

The insolent one lunged at the other, nails out and raking against his face. Then they were grappling, their movements almost too fast to follow.

Jacob appeared and leapt across the room, throwing both of them in opposite directions, slamming them into the wall on either side. He advanced at the changeling who had struck out first and, in one quick movement, slit his throat with a switchblade. He walked towards the other, his footsteps ringing hollow and making the watching changelings twitch.

"Master, please." The changeling clutched Jacob's arm. "He disobeyed you," he called out.

Jacob considered him before grabbing his hand. He carved a slow line into the changeling's wrist.

"Master, please! I was just trying to uphold your orders. He attacked me. Please."

Jacob studied him and then grinned slowly.

"Very well, James," Jacob made a cut in his own wrist and held it in front of the changeling.

"Thank you, master," the changeling looked up at Jacob in rapture, taking Jacob's wrist in his hand and drinking deeply from the wound. James pulled back shuddering, and examined his own wrist to find it whole once more. His cheeks were flushed red with blood and his eyes turned black as pitch.

Aiden's stomach dropped. Jacob wasn't a changeling in charge of the others. He had demon blood. Jacob was demonspawn, a half-demon. Aiden didn't know how it was possible. How long had it been since a powerful half-demon had walked the earth? Aiden scampered away from the window, slipping his scribe back on.

The sound of a female voice stopped Aiden short, and he crept back to the window.

"I miss exciting thing?" the woman said with a strong eastern European accent. She stood next to Jacob. Her black hair, streaked with grey, was pulled harshly away from her stern face. She looked at the dead changeling with cold disgust.

"James, dispose of this trash," Jacob said.

Arching her brow, she asked, "If he is dead, who is with girl?"

Jacob sighed heavily and pointed at another changeling, who ran off, leaving Aiden to wonder who this girl was that they were watching and why. If a demon was looking for a human, it never meant anything good.

Aiden's heart skipped a beat as he thought of Ginny, the girl Jacob had tackled at the carnival. It had seemed to be a random accident, but perhaps it hadn't been. After all, half-demons didn't just do things on accident. Not when it involved the Alliance and a Secret Keeper. Aiden leaned forward, listening closely for more information about the girl.

But the woman grew stiff and snapped her head in his direction. Aiden jumped back, heart pounding. It felt like she had looked right at him, as if she knew exactly where he was.

"Not safe to talk. Someone listens nearby," she said, answering Aiden's fears.

"Are you sure?"

"I hear his thoughts."

Aiden didn't wait to hear any more. He ran down the steps and out the back alley back to Alliance House.

Chapter 7

Ginny added the finishing touches to her painting, some purple streaks for shading and a gold highlight. It was a stylized self-portrait, her dark hair inundated with red light and golden flecks in her warm brown eyes. Her nose was straight and dainty, her lips full, and her eyebrows expressive. That was how she painted herself, and she sat back with a smile. She stretched as she looked around the room. On the far wall was a mural of an underwater scene, where a whale danced amongst starfish and seashells. The other walls were adorned with student artwork from grade school to high school, all displaying various arrays of talent.

Pat was engrossed in his project, and the look of concentration on his face meant he'd be immersed in his painting for at least another hour, if not more. She tidied up, making sure to wash all the paint off herself without ruining her clothes.

Ginny decided to wait for Pat across the street in her favorite bookshop, Parson's. It was a quiet and cozy little shop filled with lots of hidden treasures. She loved to peruse the bookshelves, looking for her next book to fall in love with. She could easily spend an hour there while she waited for Pat.

Ginny's knee ached as she crossed the street. It was a warm, sunny day and the breeze brought with it the smell of lilacs and other flowering trees. But a sharp pain jolted up her leg with each step, rankling her. She gritted her teeth and struggled to walk normally. The last thing she wanted was for someone to notice her leg was bothering her. That her knee had gotten worse instead of better. That her bruise wouldn't go away. She shook her head to clear it as she opened the door.

The tinkling of bells sounded above her head, but she wasn't prepared to find herself looking straight into Aiden's startling blue eyes. He was seated by the storefront with a book in his hands. She flushed as he took her in, his gaze calm and collected. She shut her mouth with a snap and he gave her a crooked grin, which she nervously returned, willing herself to be cool.

"What a pleasant surprise," he said, closing his book with a soft thud and standing up to greet her.

"It's Aiden, right?" she said, aiming for nonchalance as his smile disarmed her.

His grin widened. "Correct."

She felt a heady rush as she looked into his bright eyes. "Do you remember my name?"

"Of course, it's Ginny. My father's favorite kind of drink." He laughed lightly, and it transformed his features. "Does that stand for anything?"

"Evangeline. My mom shortened it to Ginny after her best friend growing up. She's always hated Eva. Too stuffy." Ginny looked down at her hands fidgeting with the hem of her shirt, unsure of what to say. It didn't help that she actually wanted to talk to Aiden. It just made her more tongue-tied.

"Do you come here often?" he asked.

She looked up and smiled. "Yes, my mom's studio is right across the street, so I come in here when I'm waiting for Pat to finish. He's painting right now."

He raised one eyebrow. "Pat?"

Her cheeks warmed. "The guy who was with me when we met. He's my best friend," she added quickly.

He set his book aside and Ginny noticed his long, slim fingers. "So you like painting?" He smiled, the sun streaming on him from the front window, haloing him in the light.

"It's fun, but I'm not the best at it," she said with a laugh. "I much prefer reading and even writing, but mom's an artist, so it's expected I'll spend my time playing with paint every now and then. Pat's the real artist out of the two of us."

He smiled broadly. "I'm sure you're better than me. Please sit down." Aiden motioned to the other arm chair. "So what do you like painting?"

"Portraits mostly. I've been playing with oils lately."

"Do you like oils?"

"Oh, I love them. Great texture and vibrant colors, and so fun to layer. I really like them, they just take forever to dry," she said, smiling and looking down at her hands. "What do you like to do?"

"Oh me? Well, I like reading." He gestured to his book with a half grin.

"I love reading!" Ginny interjected in excitement. "Sorry," she flushed as he laughed again.

"Reading is awesome. We have a huge library back at the house."

"Must be nice. Though I can come here often, it's right across the street from my mom's studio, like I said." Ginny pointed out the window. "So what's your favorite book?" she asked, looking up shyly.

"A Connecticut Yankee in King Arthur's Court."

"I love that book. It's so funny and the protagonist is so inventive and creative." Ginny laughed and Aiden joined in. Warmth blossomed in her chest, and she couldn't stop smiling.

"How about you? What's your favorite book?"

"I have a million. But I'd have to say Pride and Prejudice. I've read it at least fifteen times."

"Practical romantic, then."

She arched her brow. "Oh really?"

"With a healthy sense of humor too," he added.

"Are you done psychoanalyzing me?"

They both laughed again. Ginny liked his smile, and the way only one side of his cheek dimpled. They chatted, getting along so well she almost didn't notice Pat come out of the studio an hour later. He was on his phone and hadn't seen them yet. It struck her that she didn't want Pat to see Aiden, so she said a quick goodbye, scribbling her number down for him when he asked for it. She hopped out of the store. She was still glowing from how well they'd gotten

along, which had never happened with anyone other than
Pat before.

"All done?" she asked, catching up to Pat, breathless.
He looked up from his phone with a smile.

"Yep. All set?" He had a streak of yellow across his
cheek and blue under his jaw. Not that he would care.

"Yep, all set." They turned and began walking home,
the sun warm on Ginny's skin. She took a deep breath and
smiled at the day.

"I'm really happy with how this one's turning out.
But it's still not my favorite." He scrunched up his nose,
regarding her.

"Your favorites are a joke. They're just paintings and
sketches of me, and suddenly they're your favorites," she
said, frowning.

"My paintings of you are just extra pretty. I like them
the most," Pat said with a shrug. "You're in a good mood."

She simply nodded and smiled. Ginny liked this
feeling, this bubbly lightness. It lasted the whole day and
night. She was giddy, laughing and making jokes all day. It
stayed with her as she watched a movie and ate dinner with
Pat. It stayed with her, lifting her spirits high as she caught
up with her mom before bed. It carried her up and into her
dreams as light as a feather.

Ginny found herself on a crag of black rock above
a barren valley of cracked, desiccated earth. Clouds of
rust-colored dirt rolled across her feet and covered the
unforgiving ground. A dry, dusty wind heated the air and she
coughed as she looked around. Where in the world was she?

Closing her eyes against the dust, she had an image
flash through her mind of the face of a hideous creature.
His skin was a pallid grey and scales grew from the base of
his head down his back. He was hunched over, a black chain
wrapped around his neck, and when he smiled, Ginny saw
that he had fanged teeth. His hair was a shock of white and

his eyes were black holes that stared right through her. Chills ran down Ginny's spine as she felt bared before this nightmarish visage.

"Hello, little one," the creature spoke in a rasping voice, low and cruel, that seemed to echo through her. "Yes, I know who you are, even if you don't. I know you and the darkest thoughts that plague your little heart. The fears you conceal from the world, but cannot conceal from me. Oh, how I know you, little one."

Ginny trembled at his words and shook her head no, squeezing her eyes shut as her heart beat erratically. Who was this thing that tortured her? Just looking at him filled her with dread and an unnamable fear, and she couldn't forget his words. But how did he know so much about her? And what did he mean by saying she didn't know herself?

"I will see you soon." It was a dark promise, and Ginny watched in horror as he reached a grey hand with sharp, black talons towards her. She jumped back, opening her eyes to find herself back in the desert wasteland.

Where was she? Ginny's mind whirled as she looked around again. The valley that opened up before her was now filled with a writhing mass of black and grey forms. She knelt, leaning forward for a better look. Monsters, that's what came to mind when she saw them. Bodies warped and twisted into gruesome forms; scales covering parts of their bodies the color of corpses; horns, fangs, and talons jutting out, irregular and gruesome. Horror flooded Ginny as she watched them fight each other below her.

"My army," the voice came unbidden in her ears, and a terrible realization overtook her. There were tens of thousands of these creatures. What would an army of monsters be capable of? She broke out into a sweat and her mouth went dry at the thought. Her heart hammered in her ears and she leapt back from her crouching spot, but her foot caught on a rock and she was falling. Falling and falling while the chained monster laughed cruelly until she dreamt no more.

Chapter 8

Aiden was o the lookout for the hawk lady who had sensed his presence the last time he was watching Jacob and his men. His heart pounded as he took up his usual vantage point, his palms clammy as he pulled off his scribe. It was risky to keep up surveillance but crucial. Jackson had given him this mission for a reason, and he wasn't about to let him down. He had to figure out what Jacob was up to and why he had killed their Secret Keeper. What had Jacob learned about the Alliance? And who were they watching? It was vital he found the answer to these questions.

He wrote the same sigil on his upturned palm to be able to see and listen across distances. Focusing on the new voices he could now hear, Aiden settled down in the empty room he occupied. The smell of dust filled his nose as the floor creaked under his weight.

"She's not doing anything. What's the point in watching her?" A changeling in green complained to a changeling wearing black.

"We know where to find her and who she spends time with," the one in black answered in a bored tone. "Master can use any and all information we gather on her."

"Aren't you the good pupil?"

The changeling in black growled out a warning.

"Look, all I'm saying is my time could be better

spent."

He scoffed. "And your time is so vital?"

"We have super strength, super speed, healing abilities," the changeling in green counted on his fingers. "And I'm watching a sixteen-year-old girl draw all day? How is that a good use of my skills?"

Again Aiden wondered who they were watching and why. A flash Ginny filled his mind once again, but he pushed the image away. He couldn't make any assumptions about who they were watching. He knew nothing about that girl that would make her a target. She was special, sure, but surely not to Jacob. But he would look into the matter closely. He remembered their conversation at the bookstore with a smile. Maybe now he would even have a reason to see her again.

"Stop complaining."

Aiden's attention was drawn back to the changelings.

"I'm allowed to talk," the one in green said with a scowl.

"Talk about something else."

"I hear the book Master has is magic."

"What are you talking about?"

"He can teleport."

"Teleport?" He glared at the one in green.

"Yeah, he just writes a word down on the floor and it takes him to a different place entirely."

"Magic isn't real."

He threw his hands up in the air. "We're magic. You can't tell me you don't believe it's possible. We regenerate."

"I don't know." He rubbed his chin, but didn't stop glaring.

"The book has all kinds of magic spells in it, from what I hear."

"Then you hear too much."

The green changeling guffawed. "That's just the beginning of it. What would you do with a magic book?"

"I don't have to worry about it. I don't have one. And neither do you."

"I'm just having fun."

"It sounds like you have designs on the book. Master wouldn't like that."

"I don't have designs." The one in green crossed his

arms and slumped in his seat.

"Then give up this nonsense. You better watch yourself. That woman can read minds, I swear."

Aiden swallowed hard at the mention of the woman. He wasn't the only one nervous about her presence, it seemed. He knew Alliance members could sometimes read minds. He wondered if the same could happen to changelings. She certainly had known he was there listening last time. He shivered at the thought.

"Well, I'm on duty," the changeling in black said, standing. "Keep your mouth quiet about that book if you know what's good for you."

"Have fun watching paint dry. Great use of our time."

He left out the side door. Aiden gave him a minute before he ducked out of the building he was in and followed.

The changeling hunkered down as he walked, trying to make himself inconspicuous. Must have been hard, considering he was over six-feet-tall and built like a linebacker. He reminded Aiden of a greaser with his slicked back hair, black tee, and ripped jeans.

Aiden pretended to be on his phone as he shuffled behind the changeling. He kept his pace slightly slower than his and stayed back far enough that the changeling wouldn't notice him too much. He stayed calm as he tracked the changeling, all the way until the changeling suddenly stopped and leaned against a light pole. Aiden brushed past him and walked into the bookstore where he'd chatted with Ginny that afforded him a good look of the street. Nodding at the shopkeeper, he grabbed a book and made his way to the front of the store. He sat in one of the armchairs in the window, opening to a random page. He was really watching the changeling who was engrossed with the building across the street. The sign said Golden Ratio Studio—Ginny's mom's studio. What on earth would a changeling want with that studio? Aiden's heart sped up a beat.

They both watched their targets for an uneventful half hour. Then the studio door opened to reveal Ginny. Aiden's breathing sped up when he saw her. *Why were they watching her?* She was just as pretty as he remembered. Her hair fell in dark curtains around her face, but it gleamed red in the sunlight. She walked with the same boy from the fair. *Pat? Wasn't that what name she'd said?* They didn't even notice the changeling, even as he turned to follow them. Aiden's heart sank. He needed to learn more about her. Returning the book, he thanked the old man and slinked out into the evening.

Chapter 9

Ginny had expected her bruise, and the stabbing pain that radiated from her knee up her leg, to fade. But neither had happened. If anything, they had both gotten worse. The bruise, or mark as the hooded man from her dreams had called it, was getting darker, and lines had begun to snake up her leg like purple tendrils. And the pain was constant. It only felt better after she had dreamed of the hooded man.

Ginny had dreamt of him again last night. Again he had brushed his hand over her knee, wiping away the pain until only a dull ache remained. Again he had warned her not to trust snakes. But she didn't know anyone she couldn't trust in her life. Ginny felt like she was driving herself to distraction, trying to make sense of it all.

She found herself thinking of Aaron and the Lucky Spoon Café. Aaron was a regular down at Lucky's. He was like the dad she had never known, and he had a great knack for being around when she was having a particularly rough day. Aaron always knew what to say to cheer anyone up. He was like a Zen buddha in khaki shorts, an old t-shirt, and a baseball cap, just without the belly. His work had him travel around the world at a moment's notice, but he often brought treasures back for Ginny and Pat. He'd even spent a few Father's Days with Ginny, so she wouldn't feel left out. Aaron was just the person she could talk to about her dreams and the mark. Someone who would believe her and not think she was losing it. A walk to the diner was exactly what she needed.

She showered and dressed quickly, eager to see Aaron. He'd been gone for a particularly long stretch of time. She worried briefly that he wouldn't be there as she struggled into leggings, but quickly dismissed the thought. He was always there when she needed him. She debated inviting Pat, but she wanted to talk to Aaron about this alone. She dreaded what Pat would say about the strange things happening to her, the bruise that grew darker instead of fading, the dreams that seemed impossibly real, and the riddles the hooded man told. Whether he dismissed these things as freak occurrences or worried as much as she did about them, she wasn't up to confiding to Pat. Not until she had made some sense of things herself.

Ginny thought again of Aiden and meeting him right after getting this mark. He seemed to be a part of this all somehow, for better or for worse. Was he the snake she was warned about? That didn't quite feel right. She wondered what Aiden would say if she told him about her dreams and the mark. Would he understand what it all meant? She could see his sly grin and bright blue eyes that stared out defiantly from under his dark fringe. Ginny thought of Aiden's smile with a sort of longing and flushed. She shook her head to clear it and ran her fingers through her own dark hair, left a quick note for her mom, and headed out the door.

It was unlikely Helena Gracehurst would see the note. She was a classic workaholic who poured her soul and most of her time into her studio, scouting for artists to fill its walls or teaching classes. And most nights, after the studio had closed, she worked on her own projects. Helena was gifted and she had held onto hopes that her daughter would follow her steps. But Pat was the real artist and took classes free of charge to nurture his talent and because Ginny had practically grown up with his family. A working arrangement between two single mothers since before Pat's mom had remarried. Pat's mom had babysat Ginny after school and Helena, who had more money than she needed, would pay her, throwing in art classes for the kids and family vacations since Pat and Ginny were inseparable anyway. And Helena took them on the best trips, making up for time spent at work during time spent away, as Helena put it. Overall, Ginny felt lucky at the arrangement since Pat and his family was hers as well.

Ginny walked the familiar beat to Lucky's, texting Pat about the upcoming pottery class. Pat had really enjoyed the last class, and Ginny thought it was fun to get her hands dirty every now and then, though her final products left a lot to be desired.

Ginny pocketed her phone when she felt a sharp tap on her shoulder. She nearly jumped out of her skin, much to the amusement of the handsome stranger inexplicably seeking her attention.

"Sorry, didn't mean to startle you," he said with a crooked grin, pushing his black hair out of his grey eyes.

She placed her hand over her pounding heart. "It's okay. I need to be more aware of my surroundings." She looked down at her feet, cheeks flushed, before meeting his gaze.

He held his hand out to her. "I'm Jacob, by the way."

She shook it clumsily, face still hot. "Ginny."

"Pleased to meet you," he said with a sly smile, spinning the gold ring he wore on his left pinky.

"You too," she said, letting the silence unravel between them. He was good looking, much in the way Aiden had been, with his eyes a shocking contrast to his hair. But he was paler, colder as he smiled at her. She stood there, wondering what on Earth he could want.

A corner of his mouth turned up, "I was... wondering if you could help me."

Ginny's face went slack slightly. "Help you?"

"Yes, you see I'm new to the area, and I was hoping you could tell me a good place to grab breakfast."

"Oh sure, Lucky's is the best for breakfast or milkshakes. I'm heading there now, so I can show you the way."

"That would be great," he said and his smile transformed his classic features from a cold statue to the softness of a pale winter morning. "You can join me, my treat."

Ginny's mouth went dry at the thought and she chewed her lip. After all, she didn't know the guy. Unable to articulate the exact nature of her unease, she blurted out,

"I'm actually meeting someone already."

"They can join us, still my treat."

Ginny gave him a faltering smile and texted Pat frantically. She hardly breathed waiting for his response. He could be there in fifteen. Ginny pocketed her phone with a sigh, embarrassed to see Jacob staring at her intently.

"Pat says great. He'll meet us there."

"He?"

Ginny resumed walking to Lucky's and Jacob matched her steps. "Yes, he."

"The more the merrier," Jacob said with a shrug. He grinned at her still, and Ginny swallowed hard, looking away. "Have you lived here all your life?"

"For most of it," she said, rubbing her arm. "We moved here when I was little."

"What is there to do for fun?"

She laughed. "Not much, unfortunately. If you're old enough, there's the club on Grand."

"Are you old enough?"

Her cheeks grew hot again. "No, I'm just sixteen."

"That takes some of the fun out of it, if I can't go with you." He cast a sideways look at her.

She blinked, unsure of what to say. She had never felt so awkward before in her entire life. It didn't help that he was staring at her the whole time.

"Is Pat your boyfriend?" he asked with the hint of a smile.

"He's my best friend," she answered, crossing her arms in front of her. *What was he getting at asking something like that?* She refused to look at him, staring at the ground instead.

"There's a difference between the two."

She could hear the smirk in his voice and her anger flared up. "I'm not stupid. I'm quite aware there's a difference," she said with a scowl.

"I wasn't implying you were stupid. Forgive me."

She bristled at his apology, but decided to drop it, moving on. "When did you move here?"

"A month or so ago. My family's originally from here, and I wanted to see what it was like."

She looked up at him. "So you moved here with your family?"

"No, I'm eighteen and on my own, which is why it's great to meet you and learn more about this place," he said, giving her another sideways glance. "Make some new friends."

Ginny took a deep breath. She should be friendlier to the poor guy. She smiled brightly as they reached the diner.

"Here we are," she said, gesturing to the Lucky Spoon Café, which stood gleaming in the sun with its chrome façade. They entered and Ginny looked frantically around, but there was no Aaron to be seen, or Pat. Her stomach dropped.

Where was Aaron? He'd never been away for so long, and Ginny felt a pang of worry lance through her. Shaking these thoughts from her head, she slid into her regular booth and waited for Pat, her nerves jangling as Jacob watched her.

Jacob sat across from her, propping his elbows on the table and steepling his fingers. He flashed her a winning smile that she nervously returned. She was having a hard time making eye contact with him. His grey eyes seemed to pierce her, seeing into the secret places in her mind. He had a strong jaw and a cupid's bow mouth she tried not to look at either. Ginny ordered ginger ale to settle her fluttering stomach. She wondered why she couldn't be better at talking to strangers. Especially boys. She watched the door for Pat.

"Pat should be here any second now," she said, clearing her throat. "Any idea what you're going to order?"

He glanced up from the menu. "Full breakfast sounds good. You order anything you like. My way of saying thanks."

"There's no need for that." She smoothed a napkin on her lap.

"It's hard meeting people when you're the new kid in town. I really appreciate you showing me around."

Her shoulders relaxed as she regarded him. He looked so genuinely touched, the knot in her stomach loosened a little and she felt guilty instead. Being a stranger in a new place wasn't easy, and she kicked herself for not being friendlier. She just didn't have much experience talking with boys besides Pat and Cody, and they were practically family. She'd never had many friends outside of Pat and his circle, so she was awful at small talk. What was she supposed to do with this attractive man in front of her? She wondered if she was allergic to flirting as she rubbed her arm. Did she even want to flirt with Jacob?

"Everyone around here is nice," she said, going for unperturbed. "On the main road here, you'll find most of the good restaurants and some neat shops, so it's easy to get around downtown."

"What's your favorite restaurant?" he asked with a grin.

"The seafood place down the road. They have sushi on the weekends."

The door clanged and Ginny turned to see Pat walk in, brows furrowed and lips drawn down. She waved him over, somehow more nervous he had arrived than relieved. His thick blonde hair was disheveled and barely contained underneath his favorite hat. He plopped down next to her after a cursory nod at Jacob.

"Jacob, this is Pat. Pat, Jacob," Ginny said, introducing the two while her stomach did flip-flops. "Jacob's new in town."

Pat didn't smile and no one spoke as the waitress came to take their orders.

"I heard there's a carnival in town," Jacob said.

"Yeah, they'll be here for a few more weeks," Pat said humorlessly.

"Is it any fun?"

"Depends on if you like carnivals."

Jacob smirked in response. "How long have the two of you known each other?"

"Since I was four," Ginny said, twirling a strand of hair between her fingers. She couldn't help but look up anytime someone entered, hoping to see Aaron.

"Long time to be... friends," Jacob said.

"You make any friends here yet?" Pat asked, leaning forward.

"Just Ginny so far," Jacob said, winking at Ginny. "Which reminds me," he pulled out a pen and wrote on his napkin. "Here's my number. I'd love to go to the carnival, or sushi, with you."

Ginny turned beet red as she accepted the napkin while staring resolutely at no one. She shoved it in her pocket without looking at it. Pat scowled at the table, ripping his straw wrapper into bits. Ginny wanted to say something to lighten the mood, but couldn't think of anything. Her mind was a void, spinning like a tornado.

They waited in silence till Ginny broke it.

"So pottery two starts next week," she said, turning to Pat. She had finally thought of something to say.

"You joining too?" Pat asked her, sitting up.

Ginny talked to Pat about the upcoming class and Jacob asked her questions about art in general. Ginny found herself relaxing more as the conversation went on. When the food arrived, they all lost themselves in eating. Jacob grabbed the check when they finished, despite protests from both Ginny and Pat. He left first, asking Ginny to contact him, and leaving her to face the wrath of an angry Pat.

Pat gripped the table top and asked through gritted teeth, "What the heck was that all about?"

"I told you I ran into a stranger asking about breakfast diners, and he made me eat with him."

"What do you mean made you?" He glared at her, his usually warm brown eyes anything but friendly. Ginny found it very disturbing. She wasn't used to fighting with him.

"He insisted. I even said I was meeting someone, but he just said they could join as well."

"Why didn't you tell him to get lost?"

She crossed her arms. "That's not very nice."

Why was Pat acting this way? He never got mad, and yet here he was staring daggers at her. What had she done so wrong?

"You thought he was cute," Pat said, eyes squinting as his frown deepened.

Ginny turned three shades redder. "What?"

What on earth had gotten into Pat today? She felt suddenly drained and her knee began to ache, a dull throb that echoed in her temples.

"Oh my God, you did." He threw his hands in the air

"Well, he's not ugly. But it's not like I'm interested." Now it was her turn to glare. Couldn't he just drop the whole thing? It's not like it had inconvenienced him that much.

"Yeah, right."

"Let's just get out of here," she said, pinching the bridge of her nose.

Ginny's knee had really started to ache, probably because she had walked here. Shooting pains had started to travel up her leg, and she gratefully accepted a ride from Pat.

But despite the fact that they'd done this several times since Pat had gotten his license, this time, things were decidedly tense. Pat silently fumed and Ginny stared out the window, noticing how natural and comfortable the outside world seemed to be. It felt so alien to Ginny, not feeling at ease with Pat.

"How's Cody?" she asked, attempting to lighten the mood.

"He's at Andy's, playing video games. Andy got a new game, so he's basically lived there all week."

"I'm surprised you aren't there too," she said, turning to face Pat. He still looked disgruntled, and she sighed.

"Well, you don't play video games," he mumbled, shrugging one shoulder.

"That doesn't mean you can't."

"I did when he first got it."

She stared out the window. "It sounds fun."

"Are you really going to call that guy?" Pat asked out of nowhere, startling Ginny.

"Who, Andy?"

"No, Jacob. The guy you asked me to rescue you from." He gripped the steering wheel until his knuckles turned white.

"I don't want to," she said, rolling her eyes.

"Really?"

"I hadn't planned on it."

Pat heaved a sigh and lounged in the driver seat. He started to tell Ginny about all the clay throwing techniques he wanted to learn and practice in the new class. Ginny nodded, but couldn't escape the disquiet that gripped her. They stopped in front of her house.

Pat turned his eyes on her. "Want me to come in?"

"I actually don't feel that good. I think I just want to take a nap."

"Oh, okay. Maybe I'll head to Andy's and school them both on that game. Text me when you wake up."

"Will do."

Ginny climbed out of the car and up her porch steps. Unlocking the door, she gave Pat a small wave and hobbled up the stairs to her room, the silence echoing around her. Unsure of whether she was grateful to be alone with her disquiet, or whether she longed for her mom's hugs and a cup of cocoa, she shut the door and plopped down on her bed. Closing her eyes with a groan, she stretched out slowly and carefully, easing her leg straight. *What was wrong with her? And where was Aaron?* He could help her make sense of all this somehow. Her mother would just worry and rush her to the doctor's, and who knew what they would think of this. She began to feel drowsy, the pull of sleep tugging on her. For now, she would rest.

"Back again so soon?"

Ginny turned to see the hooded man walking towards her.

"Sorry, I didn't mean to…" she began, but he smiled at her, and she felt relieved.

"Please, sit."

He gestured to an oversized couch near the fireplace across from the loveseat. The flames danced, changing colors as they leaped and crackled. Ginny felt peaceful and energized just watching the fire.

"Fire purifies," the man said with a soft smile. She smiled back, wishing she could see his whole face, which would surely be just as beautiful as his smile. He grinned as if reading her thoughts. She sat next to him, dizzy.

"Here, let me help you," the man said, placing his hand on her aching knee.

Warmth flooded her and she sighed as he wiped away the pain, which dropped to a low throb.

"It keeps hurting."

"You have been marked for a long time, and I cannot fully heal you here, when we're not in person. There are those who can."

"Who?" she asked, rubbing her forehead.

"You've met one, a boy."

"I've met two boys since I've had this, remembering her painfully awkward encounter with Jacob today." She glanced around at the firelight glinting off the golden baubles placed around the room. But it was the family tree that drew her attention. How intricate it was. The foreign tongue it was written in.

"Not all who smile are a friend. The snake smiles to lure its prey." His voice drew her attention to him again.

"Snakes again? You must really hate them. And that doesn't help me at all because both boys smiled at me."

"Yes, but did you like them both?"

She paused to consider this. "One of them. The other, I'm not so sure."

He placed a hand on hers. "Trust your heart, my child. It will always be true. Now I must go."

"Wait, I'm confused."

"Stay strong, my child. Stay strong," he raised his hand to her eyes and she was swimming through darkness until she was pulled blissfully under.

Chapter 10

Aiden sat on the rail of the veranda, swinging his legs over the row of hedges that lined the house. Tali sat with her back to him, head leaning on the railing to look up at the stars. This was as peaceful as things got for Aiden at Alliance House and he reveled in the night that stretched out before him.

"What's going on out here?" Ari asked, shattering the peace like a sound wave. Aiden's back straightened as he looked out over the garden.

"What do you want?" Tali asked without looking up.

"Hello to you, too," Ari said.

Aiden could hear him sit down and his hands clenched involuntarily into fists at his side.

"And you two wonder why I never talk to you. So friendly." Aiden could hear Ari smirking and took a deep breath.

"Maybe we don't want to be friends with you," Tali said, sitting up and examining her nails.

"You should, you know. I'm going to be on the Council one day, and then you'll wish you were friends with me."

"You're not on the Council yet," Aiden said, spinning his legs around and standing on the veranda.

"As if I would be friends with you." Ari scoffed. "Not

55

with who you're related to."

"What are you on about now?" Talia asked, rolling her eyes.

"Oh father just told me. As if it wasn't bad enough you're a *human*." Ari made a face. "But your great-great-grandfather was also Abraham King."

"What about it?" Aiden said, cracking his knuckles, a heavy feeling in his gut.

"Oh he just disgraced his entire family by doing something so foul he was kicked out of the Keepers when he was a Secret Keeper. A Secret Keeper. Disgraced forever, just like you. Must run in the family."

"You're the only disgrace here," Tali said, giving Ari a dangerous look.

Aiden frowned. He didn't know much about his lineage since most of his family had died young, but he had to believe Ari was speaking the truth. His great-grandmother had kept the name King and passed it along to her children in remembrance of her lost family. He knew she had left the Keeper lifestyle far behind her, living amongst the normal human world after she came of age. But was there more to the story? Ari would know. His father knew everything about the Alliance and their brother organization, the human Keepers. It bothered Aiden that Ari knew more about the Kings than he did and his face burned as he faced Ari's smug smile.

"Don't worry," Ari began, "you're living up to his name. I'm sure he'd be proud of the shame you cause us daily just being here."

"Go to hell, Ari," Aiden spat out, striding off the veranda and heading for the gardens. He heard a shuffle and Ari squawked, but Aiden didn't bother to look behind him. He entered the hedges and walked towards the rose garden.

"Wait up," Tali called after him, and he paused without turning. "I punched him right in the nose," she said with a laugh as she reached him. "You should've seen his face."

"I wish I could hit him. He'd deserve it."

"You know you can't," she said softly, brushing the hair from his eyes.

He looked down on her and smiled sadly. "I know, but I'd really enjoy it."

"Well good thing for us, I can," she said with a broad grin. "He wouldn't dare get me in trouble. Next time we'll have you get a picture of it. For posterity."

"Deal," he said, smiling.

"That's better." She smiled back. "Was it true? What he just said?"

"I think so. I just hate getting a family history lesson from the likes of him." Aiden shook his head. "I knew my great-grandmother left this life behind, but I had always thought that it had more to do with the demon attacks than her father being kicked out. You know, we've had one attack each generation. First Mirabel survived, then one child each time until me. I never got the chance to hear many stories about the Kings. Other than that they all died." The truth was a bitter taste in his mouth. "And now this, that my ancestor shamed the Keepers. I wish I had been prepared for Ari's words. Maybe then I'd have been able to face him."

"Don't think that way. You're ten times—no—a hundred times better than Ari. Don't give his words any credence. You're not a disgrace—to your family or the Alliance."

Aiden looked at his best friend standing in the dark with him, her brown eyes insistent, and he could tell that she meant it. Warmth spread through him as he smiled at her and watched her return it, steady and strong. He threw his arm around her shoulders. "Thanks, Tali. You're the best."

He laughed as he watched her blush, and she hit him playfully in the ribs. "It's your bedtime," he said, letting her go.

"I don't have a bedtime," she smiled up at him.

Aiden looked up to the stars and sighed. "Well, then it's my bedtime."

Aiden said good night to Tali at the stairs. He lay in bed a long time, trying to piece together what he knew about his family. He strained for any fact he knew or had heard, adding Ari's revelation to his list. After several hours, sleep finally overtook him. But his list was still far too short.

Chapter 11

"Gin and tonic," Pat said as he strolled up to Ginny. She was waiting for him at the corner of Pine and Walnut, their usual rendezvous spot since grade school, where they had met. On her first day at her new school, they'd met at the bus stop. She could still remember feeling that small and overlooked after her mom had watched her board the bus, but Pat had befriended her. He had walked her to her homeroom so she wouldn't get lost and back to the right bus after classes. They'd been best friends ever since.

Pat brushed the hair out of his eyes and gave her his usual crooked grin. She smiled back.

"Ready to go PJs?" Ginny asked.

"You betcha."

He had a backpack slung low over one shoulder that carried his paints, pencils, and other paraphernalia he used at the studio. Plus the sketchbook he carried with him everywhere. They went to the studio a few nights a week, so Pat could work on his portfolio for art school.

They arrived, said hi to her mom and Stephanie, who was working that day, and made their way to an empty classroom. Pat set up his station and Ginny grabbed a fresh canvas, a new idea brewing in her mind.

"I've never seen you so into a painting before," Pat said, startling Ginny out of her reverie.

"I just have a clear picture of it in my head," Ginny shrugged, feeling self-conscious as Pat moved to see her work.

The smile on his lips died, and he looked down at her, brows furrowed, frowning.

"I can't believe you're painting him." Pat jabbed his finger at the portrait.

"Painting who?"

"That Aiden kid!"

She looked at her painting and was startled to see it did bear some resemblance to him. But that was no reason for Pat to lose it. "I was just painting," she said, rising from her seat. She could paint anything she wanted. Why was he glaring at her like he would murder her. So what if she even was painting Aiden? Why did that matter?

Pat dropped his face closer to her, making her squirm. "Clearly painting Aiden. So he's on your mind then?" His voice was louder than necessary.

Where was he going with this? "What are you talking about? You're being ridiculous, Pat."

"I'm being ridiculous?" his voice rose even higher. "You're the one obsessing over a guy you've only met once."

"I'm not obsessing. You are the one going ballistic." She wasn't going to correct him since she had talked to Aiden more than once. Why should she have to hide it though?

Pat's voice dropped. "I can't believe you. I thought you were better than that."

"Excuse me?" Now it was her voice that rose. "Better than what?"

"All it takes is a pretty face for you. Is that your type? Pretty, rich boys?" he said, hurling his pencil across the room. "Maybe you called that other guy, too. That creep from the restaurant."

"No, I haven't. I don't even have a type. And even if I did, it wouldn't concern you who I like or don't like or who I call!" Ginny said, anger now boiling. Not only was Pat slinging accusations her way when she hadn't done anything wrong, but she hadn't even done anything to deserve his anger. *How dare he.*

"Well, you have lousy taste," he rounded on her. "I expected more from you. You disappoint me."

"You take that back," she said, slamming down her brush. Pat's face was flushed, and she was trembling as she faced him.

"I can't take back what's true. I was wrong about you. I thought you were better than this, but you're not. You're a disappointment." Her heart dropped to her feet, leaving an awful ache in her chest.

"Then leave me alone. Because you're clearly not my friend and I'd hate to disappoint you any more. So why don't you get out of my life and stop telling me what to do," she said before she turned and fled the room. She wiped hot tears away as she ran outside in shock. She had never been this angry before—never even fought with Pat about anything other than which movie to see. *But he had taken it too far. How could he say those things about her? He was supposed to be her best friend. How was she a disappointment? How could he say that? All over a painting?*

After a few blocks, the pain in her knee flared up and she had to slow down, but she was intent on keeping one foot in front of the other. The sun had set and twilight trickled in, bringing the stars with it. The dark deepened, and Ginny felt uneasy as she moved from one halo of yellow light to another, traveling under the street lights.

A couple blocks from home was a street of now-closed shops. Cheery enough during the day, they had taken on an empty and hungry look in the night. As she passed them, their eyes followed her. She shivered, keeping her gaze resolutely in front of her.

A figure stepped out from an alley and Ginny jumped, her heart hammering in her chest. He was swathed in shadows and Ginny couldn't make out his face. She halted, a cold sweat breaking out on her neck.

"Little late to be out walking on your own," the man said, stepping into the light. It was Jacob, she registered with a shock. The shadows from the lamp distorted his features, making them look grotesque. His grin stretched too thin under hollow eyes, and Ginny wondered how she had ever found his cruel looks attractive. His smile glinted dangerously as he took another step towards her.

"It's Friday night. I don't turn into a pumpkin at nightfall," she said in a too-small voice.

"And thank goodness for that." Every word sent

another chill through her. "I'd like to take you somewhere now, will you come?"

Her mind revolted. The last thing she wanted was to go anywhere with him. She took a few steps forward. "I can't, sorry. I'm already late for my curfew, and I can't afford to get in trouble."

He raised a brow and strode towards her. "Surely you wouldn't get in trouble if your mom isn't home to catch you."

"How would you know if she's home or not?" His smile paralyzed her.

"Look, you can make this easy or difficult," he said, snapping his fingers. Five dark silhouettes emerged from the gloom.

"I had hoped you would call me, Ginny. Then all of this wouldn't have been necessary. Now I have to be, well, persuasive, and it's really all your fault."

She backed away from him, heart pounding in her chest. "Just leave me alone." Her hands started to shake as she brought them up close to her chest. *This couldn't be happening. Not in real life.*

Ginny spun around, looking for a way to escape as the men circled closer. Malice shone in their black eyes and their teeth were bared like jackals. Ginny's heart pounded frantically as one man lunged towards her. Her body reacted and she twisted out of the way. She ducked past two others until she was grabbed roughly from behind. Panic rose in blinding waves as she struggled to break away.

She bucked and kicked. "Let go of me," she shrieked. The grip on her went slack and she fell forward, hitting the pavement hard. She looked up to see Aiden standing over the now-unconscious man holding what looked like a billy club. *What was he doing here?* Ginny felt dizzy just looking at the club, and a sharp stab of pain lanced upward from her knee to her side.

"Are you okay?" Aiden asked, his face haloed in the light, concern etched into his blue eyes.

All she could do was nod. Aiden held the club up as one guy charged him, bringing it down hard on the man's head, and he slumped to the ground unconscious. The other three rushed Aiden at the same time and he ducked and swerved, dodging blows so quickly Ginny's head spun. He used his club to knock the wind out of one man with a jab to his solar plexus before spinning and knocking out another. The club rose again and came down hard to crack the ribs of one man, before swinging up again to knock both remaining men out.

Aiden twirled the club in his hand, turning to face Jacob who stood there, spinning the ring on his hand with a strained nonchalance. Aiden tossed the club from one hand to the other and drew out a shimmering sword. The world tilted and another wave of pain and nausea coursed through her. Ginny seriously wondered if she would have the joy of throwing up on the street to add to this wonderful evening's charming events.

"You know what this is, don't you Jacob?" Ginny heard Aiden say through the blearing pain she felt in her head. She opened up her eyes to see Jacob spit in return. "Backup is on the way. There's no way you can win this fight."

Jacob sneered at Aiden, hate written across his features. "You'll regret this, boy." He gave Aiden one more withering look, then turned, running into the night.

"Are you okay? You don't look so good," Aiden said, crouching beside her. Ginny reached for his hand, but it felt like she was swimming through sludge and she couldn't manage it. A voice spoke up in the back of her mind, insisting and firm. She had to tell him something, she had to tell him.

"I've been marked." She couldn't remember what this meant, but she had to tell him. He had to understand.

"Where?" Aiden said, shaking her, but she was so tired. "Where?" He insisted.

"My knee," Ginny tried to gesture, but the world and Aiden were both telescoping away from her, and she was swallowed up by the black night.

Chapter 12

Aiden watched in horror as Ginny slumped unconscious to the ground. He belted his tonfa and sword with the bitter knowledge that they were harming Ginny. Yanking his scribe over his head, he marked a quick healing sigil on her upturned palm. He prayed that would be enough to get her to Alliance House.

He picked her up in his arms and briskly hurried home, slinging her slightly over his shoulder for a better grip. She was far too pale, her eyelids fluttered as if she was dreaming, and her hair fell in dark curtains, a stark contrast to her skin.

"Jackson," Aiden shouted as he burst into the Alliance House. "Jackson, come quick."

Jackson appeared on the stairwell. His brow creased as he took in a panting Aiden holding Ginny.

"She's been marked."

"Get her to the infirmary, now."

Aiden rushed up the stairs, Ginny had started to moan in pain, her breathing growing ragged.

"Where's Lionel?" Aiden asked, looking around frantically for their healer.

"He stepped out."

"Where?" His voice went high as he met Jackson's eyes. Jackson turned and led Aiden into the infirmary.

"Do not worry, Aiden. I can help her."

"Of course you can," he said, a rush of relief flooded through him as he spoke the words. He lay Ginny on the examining table in the middle of the room.

Jackson dipped his hands in holy water and sprinkled some on Ginny's face. She stilled.

"Where is she marked?"

"Her knee," Aiden pointed where Ginny had gestured right before she fainted.

Jackson used scissors to cut away the bottom of Ginny's pants and revealed an angry welt with mottled lines of poison climbing up her leg.

Jackson inhaled sharply when he saw the mark and signed the cross over Ginny. He pulled off his scribe and began to write sigils over the mark. The golden lines melted into the mark, erasing it bit by bit. Jackson sang a healing song as he worked. to strengthen his healing marks. Finally, the last hint of the mark had disappeared and Ginny sighed, her breathing soft and steady.

"She is weak, but she willl be fine now. Lionel can administer healing draughts."

"Thank God," Aiden said, eyes never leaving Ginny's face.

"Who is she, Aiden? How did she come to bear the mark?"

"Her name is Ginny. Jacob marked her before I knew he was a demon spawn. He bumped into her at the carnival and knocked her over. I thought it was just an accident then. But that must have been when he marked her, then he was watching her. I'm so stupid for not figuring it out. He tried to kidnap her tonight. He marked her for a reason."

"Do not be too harsh on yourself," Jackson said, clamping his hand over Aiden's shoulder.

Aiden's eyes met Jackson's. "I thought she was just a normal girl. I had no idea she was angelborn."

"Surviving the mark proves she is angelborn. I have never seen a mark as bad as that before."

"She's had it for weeks."

"She is lucky she survived, especially around you. Your blessed weapon and scribe would have caused a surge in the demon mark, poisoning her rapidly."

Aiden grimaced and turned away, Jackson's hand

falling back to his side. "I had to. Jacob tried to kidnap her tonight. I was able to stop him and his changelings from getting her, but Jacob escaped."

"Why would Jacob go to all this trouble to get this girl? That is the question we must answer. She is somehow the key to all this. What is her full name?" Jackson asked, turning to look at Ginny closely.

"Ginny Gracehurst. Actually, Ginny is short for something. Her real name is—"

"Evangeline," Jackson said in a whisper. "Of course." He rubbed his jaw as he took in Ginny's sleeping figure.

"What?" What was going on here?

"She's not just angelborn, Aiden. She's not just any descendant of the angel, the angel is her father."

"Gracehurst. I should have known!"

"She is here safe because of you. Do not forget that. I must attend to a few things. Let me know the moment she wakes."

Jackson retreated to the library where he spent his time the most. Aiden stayed next to Ginny's bed, afraid she somehow wouldn't survive the mark, after all.

He watched her as she slept, taking in the fine lines of her face, the blossoming color beginning to return to her cheeks, her dark brown hair that gleamed red in the light, as though her hair was made of hidden flames. Aiden tried to recall what color her eyes were, and an image of her with chocolate-brown eyes flecked with gold as she smiled popped into his head. She looked deceptively delicate with her slim build and porcelain features, but he knew she must be undeniably strong and fierce to have survived the mark as long as she did and completely unaided.

"We have a guest, I see," Lionel said, entering the room with his hands laden with supplies for the infirmary.

"She was marked," Aiden rushed to explain.

"She just needs some restorative draughts and she'll be back to normal," Lionel said as he put away supplies. His voice was low and calm, like molasses.

"Can I help?"

Lionel looked taken aback, but nodded.

"Grab these," he said, scribbling on a notepad. He handed Aiden a list of the herbs needed, before stopping to check Ginny's vitals and examine her knee. She would have a pretty cool scar from the encounter.

The walls were lined with shelves laden with different herbs and oils. Aiden gathered the ones he needed in silence. His hands shook slightly as he measured things out, remembering how Ginny had collapsed in his arms while trying not to spill anything that would help her recover. He had been the reason she passed out at all, with his blessed weapons. Pangs of guilt tore through him. This was his fault. He should have known who she was days—no weeks—ago. He should have protected her. He should have helped her. How much had she suffered because he hadn't connected the dots and saved her sooner? And who knew how close she came to an even worse fate. These thoughts tormented him as he worked. Ginny slept peacefully on, and he kept her in his sights as he worked around the room.

Later, Aiden watched as Lionel administered another draught to Ginny. She sighed in her sleep, looking peaceful. Her color had fully returned, especially her lips were a rosy pink in the light.

"That should do it," Lionel said with a smile.

Aiden rubbed his tired eyes and stretched. "When do you think she'll wake up?"

"Probably tomorrow. She just needs rest now."

Aiden nodded and began cleaning up, putting back the herbs and oils they had used, cleaning the vials, and wiping down the tables. He liked to keep Ginny in view as he worked his way around the room. Seeing her sleeping carefree was like its own restorative draught for him. But guilt still weighed him down, and he kept an eye on her, afraid her condition would suddenly deteriorate if he left. Long after Lionel had wandered out of the infirmary, Aiden sat next to Ginny's bed and watched her sleep.

"You're still here?" Tali asked, bursting into the room full of bluster. He could sense her temper flaring even without her shouting.

She threw her long braids over her shoulder and stared at him with pursed lips, an eyebrow raised.

"Keep quiet, she's sleeping," Aiden said with a frown. He angled himself so he could still see Ginny now that Tali stood in the way.

Tali rolled her eyes. "Exactly, so why are you still here?"

Aiden gritted his teeth, then relaxed. "I want to make sure she's okay."

"Dad said she's just fine now. Out of danger and all that," Tali said, examining her nails, her jaw tight.

"I'd still like to make sure."

"You don't believe my dad?" she asked loudly, giving him a long, cold look that put Aiden on edge. Why did she have to bother him now? He was already stressed enough without another interrogation.

"No, it's not that." He rubbed his arm, avoiding Tali's gaze. "I just feel responsible."

"Nonsense. And besides, you barely know her."

"She's not completely a stranger. We've met."

"When?"

"A couple of times," he said with a shrug. He didn't like this line of questioning.

"When you've been gone on your secret mission you can't tell me about?"

"Yes," he said, and it was his turn to roll his eyes.

"I still can't believe you won't tell me what's going on."

"You know I'm not allowed to talk about it," he said. Tali shifted her weight from one foot to the other, arms crossed and glaring at him. He wished she would just let all of this go for once. Why did she have to be so annoyingly stubborn? Nothing stopped her, not even Jackson's talk with her.

Her face softened a little. "I hate you keeping secrets. And now she's part of that secret. I wish she hadn't come here." Her lips pursed, and she glanced behind her at the sleeping Ginny darkly.

"Well, I had to bring her here."

"All I know is you won't leave her side. Why is that exactly?" She trained her eyes on him again.

"I told you. I feel responsible for what happened to her."

"You're lying to me."

"I am not," he said with a squeak.

Her hands fell to her hips and she leaned towards him. "You like her, don't you?"

"She's a good person."

"Oh my God, you do," she said, crossing her arms

again, leaning back with her face flushed.

"Stop it, Tali." Aiden ran his hand down his face.

"How well do you even know her?"

"Will you drop it?"

"Not until you stop your stupid bedside vigil."

He emphasized each word as he sat up again. "I'm not doing anything."

"Then leave the room."

"No."

"You're an idiot. Keep your stupid vigil. I'm leaving," Tali said as she stomped off.

Aiden rubbed the back of his neck as he tried to calm his breathing. Tali was his best friend, but she knew how to make him angry. He took a few deep breaths as he watched Ginny sleep. Her breaths came softly, her hands curled near her cheek. Watching her sleep so peacefully, surely all must be okay.

Chapter 13

Ginny was flying through the air, the wind rustling her hair behind her as she laughed, passing blazing pink and sunrise-orange tinted clouds. She was soaring over the town and Lake Locke loomed ahead of her, but centuries old and untouched by man. It was surrounded by an ancient forest. She landed on the banks and looked at the towering trees that bordered the sands.

A voice filled her head, clear and insistent.

"In the early days, God sent two angels to earth to teach humans about the divine. They were his two brightest."

Two angels rose out of the lake without leaving even a ripple across its calm waters. They gleamed under the sun, a golden light emanating from their porcelain skin. One had red-gold hair and looked familiar to Ginny, though she couldn't place him. The other had pure gold hair. Tall and formidable, they stretched iridescent multi-colored wings, like mother of pearl. Bowing to each other, they went off in separate directions.

"And so they went to teach the different tribes of the ways of the creator, and they performed miracles in His great name. But the humans were in awe of the angels and tried to make them into gods themselves. The angel called Grace chastised them, and from him they learned about God and were given gifts of knowledge to improve their lives." Ginny saw the

angel with red-gold hair writing on parchment in front of a group of men. She recognized sigils amongst another language. She could sense that they were far from the lake, in another country. The other language must have been their native tongue.

"But the other angel called Shemiazaz was flattered by being called a god and didn't stop the humans from worshipping him. They brought him gifts of wine and women, and he punished those who did not do his bidding, becoming more and more corrupt. Finally, after murdering an innocent, Shemiazaz was so corrupted he transformed. Heavenly fire engulfed him in gold tongues of flame, but instead of purifying him, he was judged and burned. His skin charred, turning corpse-grey, his feathered wings turned black and leathery, razor-sharp talons sprouted from his fingers, and what had once been achingly beautiful to behold was made hideous. God punished him by keeping him prisoner in the depths of Tartarus, the deepest pits of perdition." Ginny saw the transformation, saw his skin turn grey and scaly, saw him rake his claws against his stone cage in Tartarus, as chains of darkness snaked around him. He let out a coarse scream that rattled the enclosed rock walls, but the darkness swallowed all.

"Shemiazaz had already made changelings, those humans who had drunk his blood and were changed themselves, and these changelings became the first demons. Shemiazaz still controlled them, for he was powerful and could enter the minds of his changelings and men.

"Far from repenting, he has plotted his revenge, and desires above all else to be released from his prison. His power is undiminished, as evil as it had been pure. He enters the minds of men and bids them to do his evil work in defiance of God. He is biding his time, but the time for him to make his move is fast approaching."

The voice that had grown so ominous and cold at this declaration sent shivers coursing through Ginny. She had another awful image of Shemiazaz chained in the pits beyond hell. The sight of him made her tremble, and an icy fear gripped her.

But a feeling of peace spread and thawed her as the voice spoke again, now light and full of love.

"You will not be alone. You will not be unaided in your hour of need. The strength of God and of his servants will be *with you.”*

Ginny was filled with an unnamable bliss as she was lifted into the air again.

“Remember this door between worlds and remember the doom of Shemiazaz and his follies.”

She was lifted higher into darkness and slept undisturbed.

Ginny was surprised to find herself in a strange, white room with Aiden slumped over, sleeping in a chair when she woke. She had no idea where she was, or how long she had even been sleeping. She pulled back the covers and gasped, as she saw that her pants had been cut open and the mark on her knee was gone. All that remained was a diamond-shaped scar. It was too bad about the jeans, they were one of her favorites, but she tested out her leg and laughed as she found the pain was completely gone.

Aiden stirred and smiled at her shyly as he rubbed his eyes.

“Good morning,” Aiden said. “Well, good evening at least.”

“How long was I asleep?”

“About a day. How are you feeling?”

“A day? My mom is going to kill me,” she said, sitting up in a hurry, feeling a rush in her head at the sudden movement.

“She knows you’re here,” Aiden reassured her.

Ginny felt a little dizzy and fell back on the bed, trembling.

Aiden handed her a mug of what looked like tea. “Here, drink this.” Ginny took a drink and was surprised by the taste, like honey melting on her tongue. Soon she had drained it all.

“Feel better?”

“Yes,” she said, feeling a little self-conscious.

“It’s good to see you awake again,” Aiden said with a

warm smile.

Ginny blushed as he stood. Suddenly she remembered Jacob trying to grab her with his men last night. *What on earth was going on?*

"I'll just go and get Jackson," he said while leaving.

Ginny wasn't sure who Jackson was and a rush of anxiety flooded her. Her palms felt sweaty. *What had happened to her exactly?* Her nerves jangled with uncertainty.

Aiden returned with a middle-aged Asian man with salt-and-pepper hair kept short and tidy.

"Hello, I am Jackson," he said in a gentle voice.

"I'm Ginny."

"Yes, I imagine you have some questions." He looked to Aiden. "Aiden, would you mind?"

"I'll just be outside then."

Ginny watched Aiden leave with a mixture of relief and trepidation, finding herself alone with this stranger in a strange place. But Jackson gave her a welcoming smile, and she felt better.

"Let me first say that you are in a safe place." He spread his arms wide, sitting in Aiden's chair.

"What is this place?"

"We are called the Alliance. I run the chapter here. The Alliance is a world-wide family."

"I've never heard of it."

Jackson fidgeted with his glasses, cleaning them on his shirt, and continued. "We are a secret organization."

"What do you do?"

"We protect humans from demons. It is our sacred mandate," he said, folding his hands together in his lap. Ginny wasn't sure she'd heard him right.

"Demons?" she said with a laugh before her dream returned to her. "Like Shemiazaz? I dreamt of him."

His mouth dropped open for a minute before he continued, "You have had prophetic dreams?"

Ginny blushed. "I don't know about all that, but I've had strange dreams ever since I got marked."

"Tell me about them, please."

"There was a hooded man who helped ease the pain in my knee. And then last night, I dreamt about two angels who came to earth. Shemiazaz was one of them. He turned into a demon, didn't he?" she asked with a shiver, remembering the demon's face.

"Yes, he and the angel called Grace came to teach men and enrich their lives. Shemiazaz took a darker path and became the first of the greater demons who had even taken mortal women as wives.

"Grace stayed pure, though he had fallen in love with humanity, and with one woman in particular. Shemiazaz was imprisoned in Tartarus, in perdition, but his children and his changelings were attacking innocents. Grace spoke to God about this injustice."

"What happened?" she asked, sitting up.

"God told Grace to live on Earth and take a wife. He said Grace and his descendants would be charged with keeping mortals safe. The Alliance was created out of descendants of the angel, or angelborn as we call them. We work to keep people safe from demons and changelings."

"What are changelings?" She cocked her head, trying to wrap her mind around the stories this stranger was telling her.

"You would know them as vampires. But they do not feed on human blood; changelings need demon blood. It strengthens them, giving them superhuman speed and strength, and regenerative powers that prevent them from aging. But they are cursed. They obey their demon master, and upon death, become demons themselves."

"So demons are real?" Ginny asked with a shiver, her mind spinning at the thought.

"Yes, Jacob himself is half-demon, and a powerful one at that. The mark you bore was demonic."

"What does Jacob want from me?" she asked, hugging herself. She could still see Jacob standing in the light of the streetlamp, his icy, grey eyes glinting as he looked at her hungrily. Remembering his maniacal grin was enough to give her the chills.

"That, we can only speculate for now. Why he marked you is a little easier. An angelborn who bears a demon mark will have stronger, purer angelic powers, regardless of bloodline. But it is very dangerous to the angelborn and is forbidden because it can prove to be fatal."

"So Jacob wanted me to have stronger powers?"

"So it would seem." He clasped his hands together, regarding her with a curious expression.

Ginny shook her head. "But I don't have powers. I'm not some superhero."

"You are angelborn. The powers are in your blood."

Ginny struggled not to roll her eyes. "How do you know that for sure? I don't even know anything about my dad. He died when I was three."

"You bore the demon mark. That alone is proof enough. And I believe we know a great deal about your father."

"You know who my father was?" She perked up, staring at him and waiting for his answer while her heart seemed to beat in her ears. She finally had a chance to hear about her dad.

"I know who he is."

Silence spun around them as her ears burned. "Is?" She scoffed. Surely she hadn't heard him right.

He paused and examined her as her heart pounded. "He is the angel called Grace."

She shook her head, heart pounding. "That's not possible."

"Your last name is Gracehurst, the name the angel is known to take this century."

"My dad is dead," she hugged herself closer, refusing to meet Jackson's gaze.

"Your dad cannot die."

Ginny felt she had been submerged in water. Jackson's voice was far away and small, and her breath caught in her chest. She closed her eyes, trying to recall anything about her father. She had last seen him when she was three. When he had died. She couldn't remember anything—not his smile, not his voice, nothing—and her hands curled into fists at her side.

"Then where has he been all these years?" she asked through clenched teeth.

"I do not presume to know the angel's affairs," Jackson answered, squirming in his seat. He took off his glasses and cleaned them with a corner of his shirt again.

"I'm not allowed to ask why my dad abandoned me?"

"I simply meant that I am not the one to answer that question. The angel does everything for a reason. I do not presume to know them."

"Where is he?" She slapped her hand down on the

bed.

"Again, I am afraid I do not know."

"Doesn't he come here to help you guys?" Ginny reached up and angrily wiped the tears from her eyes. Her mind was buzzing, and over and over she asked herself, *how he could he have left her, how could her mother have lied to her, how could her entire life be a lie?*

"He has not, well, graced us with his presence in decades. Though he may do so now that you have found your way to us. He has visited his children before."

"I can't believe this," Ginny said, pressing her hands to her eyes.

"Believe what?"

"I've been lied to my whole life." Her voice trembled, threatening to break as she tried to hold the tears back.

"I am sure it was done for a reason. Your mother can explain better than I can when she arrives." Jackson cleared his throat and checked his watch. He frowned at the time.

"When she arrives?" Ginny asked, dropping her hands.

"She should arrive shortly."

"I can't believe this." Her mind swirled and anger rushed through her, making her warm.

"It is a lot to take in, I know."

Her cheeks flushed and her whole body felt hot. Her hands were trembling and she pushed them against her thighs to steady them as her pulse pounded in the base of her throat.

"Do you know?" Her voice was growing louder and she couldn't stop it. "Do you know what it's like to think your dad is dead?" The power of the word stopped her short as always, but her anger flared up again and she continued. "Thought he was dead almost your entire life...." And now her voice rose an octave. "Now you tell me he's been alive this whole time? That all the pain and suffering and hurt was for nothing?"

She choked and a silence fell between them as Jackson fidgeted with his glasses, looking everywhere but at her. She huffed, pressing her hands together as she tried to control the riot of emotions tumbling through her.

"I understand that—" Jackson began, looking at her again.

"Do you?" she interrupted, glaring at this meticulous stranger. How could he possibly understand how she felt just now? She hardly knew how she felt.

"Yes, I do." Jackson kept her gaze.

He looked so uncomfortable, Ginny felt guilty. She didn't mean to berate him, he hadn't lied to her for her entire life. She sighed, deflating, and wiped away the tears that had escaped, sniffling. "I'm sorry, I shouldn't be taking this out on you." She took a couple of deep breaths before looking up at him again.

"You would not be the first." He gave her a small smile.

Pushing questions of her father from her mind, a dozen others rose to take its place. "So Alliance members are all descendants of the angel. So everyone here is related?"

"Everyone except Aiden. He is not angelborn. Most members are only distantly related to the angel. However, Angel blood can never be diluted, and can be activated no matter how far removed one is. Although you will have considerably stronger powers than many here, due to the demon mark and your natural abilities. And it can never carry a taint. Most Alliance members do not consider themselves as relatives. Angel blood is never impure, so most only consider their mortal lineage when dating."

Ginny flushed as Jackson explained this. She wanted to change the subject.

"What kind of powers will I have? I've never had any before."

"They remain latent until you come into contact with a demon. You would not have noticed them before. Now, with training, you will be a great fighter. Angels are great warriors, after all. You may also show a proclivity to healing. Those are the two most common abilities angelborn possess."

Ginny preferred this line of questioning. This was safer to discuss, to consider. She took a deep breath and smoothed down her shirt. "Why would Jacob need me to have those powers?" she asked, raising her eyes.

"It is difficult to guess," Jackson said, staring at her closely. Ginny squirmed under his scrutiny until he blinked and his gaze relaxed.

"He's still out there," she said quietly.

"We will keep you safe."

"What about my mom?" Ginny's stomach twisted.

He frowned, glancing at his watch. "She should have been here by now."

"What if Jacob's gotten to her?" Ginny asked, springing suddenly from the bed, shuffling to get her legs free in time to steady herself. Panic coursed through her as she thought of her mom in Jacob's hands. He had tried to kidnap her, there was no saying what else he was capable of, and a cold sweat broke out over her at the thought.

"There is no reason to suspect that, but we can send someone to your house."

"She won't be home; she'll be at the studio. We have to go get her right now," Ginny shouted.

"You think she is in danger?" he asked, looking at her closely.

"She's never late to stuff like this. This is the woman who wants to take me to the ER for scraping my knee, let alone a demon mark. She wouldn't be late coming to see me after what happened."

"Very well..." Jackson began.

"I'm coming with you." Ginny struggled to keep her voice low and even, to slow her ragged breathing.

Jackson shook his head. "We must keep you safe."

She met his gaze. "This is my mother."

"It will be dangerous, and you are untrained."

"I'm going," Ginny said, now openly glaring at Jackson. She refused to look away from him.

After a few minutes he spoke. "You will stay by my side at all times. Do you understand me?"

"Yes."

She felt a rush of relief that she had gotten her way. She couldn't just sit by and wait for someone else to help her mom. But as she thought of what possibly lay ahead of her, that a half-demon could be waiting for her, it made her palms clammy and an icy chill traveled down her spine.

She followed Jackson out of the room to where Aiden waited for them.

"Belt up and find something for Ginny to utilize. We are finding out what is keeping Mrs. Gracehurst."

Aiden nodded and headed down the hall and down the stairs.

"You're coming with us?" Aiden asked Ginny, eyebrows raised.

"Of course. It's my mom." She hurried to keep up with him, her steps echoing his.

"It might be dangerous."

She bit her lip for a moment. "My magical blood is supposed to help with that." She concentrated on her feet making each step, despite her trembling. Then they were on the first floor.

"I'm surprised Jackson agreed to this."

"He can't really stop me from going." They passed room after room on the first floor until Aiden came to a stop.

"Well then, you'll need a few things from here."

They had reached a huge gymnasium full of weapons of every kind and make, studding the walls and set up in training stations everywhere. The metal shone with a soft light, just like Aiden's sword had the night Jacob tried to kidnap her.

Aiden walked up to a station filled with gleaming swords and the billy-club he had wielded against Jacob and his men.

"This is a tonfa. I use it for defense, along with this," he said, holding up a sword that looked much too heavy to Ginny. "The wood bears the Angelic script so it works as a shield and a way to incapacitate demon spawn. The sword is made of aoiveae; a blessed metal we forge all our weapons from."

"What does it say?" she asked, examining the burnished symbols. She had never seen anything quite like it before, well except in her dreams. She remembered the family tree being written in something similar.

"They're sigils, words in the Angelic tongue that we use. These are for protection, speed, agility, and lightness. We use sigils for healing, protection charms, even to see and hear across distances. All sorts of stuff."

She laughed nervously. "Sounds like magic."

"It comes in handy. Here, see how this feels," he said, handing her a short sword. She held it straight in front of her, looking down at the weapon in her clumsy hands with dismay. "It feels awkward. I don't even know how to hold this."

They tried a few more, until she found one she felt

more comfortable holding. Her fear was beginning to rise like bile in the back of her throat. Was she really prepared to face men like the ones who had tried to kidnap her again? But she was worried for her mother, praying she was safe despite Ginny's fears. That this rescue mission was for nothing.

"We might not need them," Aiden said, handing her two small knives and seeing her expression.

Her eyes met his. "But we might."

"Jackson and I will be there to protect you."

She swallowed past the lump in her throat and nodded. "I just hope my mom's okay."

"Let's go and make sure she is," Aiden said. He clasped her shoulder and gave it a reassuring squeeze.

Chapter 14

Aiden turned to see Ginny staring at her mother's studio, her face pale and drained of color. The entrance was a gaping maw; the doors had been ripped clean off their hinges. The twisted metal was scattered across the ground. The studio was dark, save for a light in the hallway just outside the front room and a flickering candelabra along the back wall. Aiden took Ginny's hand in his, feeling her tremble. He ran his thumb across the back of her hand, so small in his.

"I'm right here next to you," Aiden said, meeting Ginny's eyes.

Jackson turned to survey the two of them, his face grave but confident as he met Aiden's eyes.

"I will be point. Aiden, you bring up the rear. Ginny, you stay behind me at all times," Jackson said. "We have to keep Ginny safe at all costs. Understood?"

They nodded and scurried after Jackson as he headed toward the studio. The front room was a gallery. The wide, open gallery and strewn pedestals and broken statues looked sinister in its darkened state. It was empty; the candlelight cast long shifting shadows and glittered off broken glass on the floor. Unearthly light and flickering shadows filled the room. Feeling exposed, Aiden followed Jackson in, careful to muffle his steps.

Jackson drew his swords, the aoiveae blades letting

off a soft, silver glow. Aiden unbelted his tonfa and motioned for Ginny to pull out her sword. Aiden was glad to see there were no signs of blood, when a loud banging at the end of the hall made them all jump. It was a hollow sound like a mallet pounding on wood. Jackson crouched and peered down the hall. The pounding continued.

"Open up, love," a man called tauntingly.

Bang

"We won't hurt ya."

Bang

"We just need you for bait."

Bang

The laughter of several others joined his. Ginny was shaking visibly, but Aiden felt his body go rigid. Jackson gestured to him and Aiden sidled next to him. At the end of the hall a man stood laughing as he watched what transpired in the other room. The banging hammered out again, echoing and unraveling down the hallway towards them. Aiden could hear the laughs and taunts of several men in the room, but he knew how to draw them out. They had better odds fighting in the open of the front room. Pulling out one of his aoiveae knives, he said a silent blessing, took careful aim, and released, watching the knife go end over end before lodging in one man's throat as he turned to face them. He fell with a thud.

Aiden ducked back into the gallery, followed by Jackson. They hurried Ginny behind them as the sound of footsteps thundered towards them. Aiden unsheathed his sword, the blade a gleaming arc of pale light in one hand and the tonfa spinning around his other hand to shield his arm. Aiden risked a glimpse of Ginny behind him before five men burst into the room with a cry. They held dulled machetes; their black eyes and the flush of blood on their chalk-white faces marked them as changelings with demon blades. He had to keep Ginny safe. Aiden grimaced, bracing himself for a difficult fight. It was all he had time to think of before the changelings charged. Two of them engaged Aiden immediately, and he found himself under a barrage of attacks.

Jackson fought to the right of him, moving blurs of color and the sound of metal clanging the backdrop to Aiden's racing heart. No matter what, he had to keep Ginny safe. This thought spurred him on as a changeling brought his blade down hard. Aiden parried his blow, and the other joined in, slicing upwards toward him. Aiden blocked it with difficulty. Changelings had supernatural strength from the demon blood they drank, and these two were freshly charged. The dark luster of their weapons marked them as poisonous, and Aiden knew better than to let one get close to him. Aiden dipped and ducked and swung at them with all his might, hoping to defeat them before his strength faltered. It was all he could do to block and slash as the changelings jumped and darted—like shadows—in and out of reach. But Aiden was well trained with his weapons, and he let his body react to each blow. Finally, a well-placed feint and strike found its mark, and one changeling fell to the floor with a shriek.

A quick look around showed a body in front of Jackson, who was trying in vain to engage the other two changelings. One had broken off of him and stood before Ginny, who trembled before him as she held her sword out in shaking hands. The sight enraged Aiden, and he turned and attacked the last changeling before him with a fresh surge of energy, putting his strength into each strike. Aiden went on the offensive, hacking at the changeling again and again. The changeling shoved Aiden back and with a cry, brought down its machete with a clash that resonated down to Aiden's bones. And still there was the constant pounding down the hall. Ginny needed him. He slashed upwards and sent his opponent's machete to the floor with a clatter. Another slice silenced the changeling.

Aiden spun around to see Ginny, her lip swollen and bleeding, and was about to run to her when a scuffle in the hallways got his attention. A changeling stepped into the room holding a knife to Mrs. Gracehurst's throat. He bared his teeth at them.

"Now, no more funny business. We take the girl and her dear ole mum and we leave. Understood?"

"We will never agree to that," Jackson said, raising his sword. The changeling in front of him lunged at Jackson and the two wrestled for control.

"Enough." The changeling holding Ginny's mom threw his knife at Jackson, but missed. Mrs. Gracehurst saw her opportunity and tried to break away from him, but he grabbed her arm with a growl. His hand went to her throat. She struggled against him, but her face turned a mottled red. He lifted her up into the air and she kicked her feet, desperate for air. Jackson broke free of the changeling's grip and sent the changeling flying. Unfortunately, the changeling landed on the candelabra which crashed to the floor, the flames finding purchase and flaring up along the wall.

Ginny's mom continued to struggle, but grew weaker and weaker as the fire spread behind her, a scene from a nightmare. Ginny dropped her sword with a clatter.

The whole room filled with light and Aiden thought someone must have turned on the lights to the room, but when he turned to look, he saw that the light was emanating from Ginny. Her eyes glowed a molten gold and her hair whipped behind her in a red gleam, as though she was wrapped in wind. The air crackled and a desert breeze blew dusty heat that filled the room.

The changeling fell to his knees at Ginny's feet, screaming as he clawed at his skin. Aiden felt the buzz of an unseen force pass him, and the other two joined in, shrieking and contorting. The changeling holding Mrs. Gracehurst dropped her, doubling over and howling. All three fell to the floor twitching, before they inexplicably stopped moving at the same time with a final, shuddering gasp. Mrs. Gracehurst gulped air down as the sprinkler system showered them with water. The fire guttered and went out.

Ginny trembled, the golden light leaving her, and she slumped to the floor. They rushed to her side, and she looked at all three of them with tears in her eyes.

"Are you alright?" Ginny said, her voice shaking.

"You saved us," her mom said, engulfing Ginny in her arms, her voice raw and strained, but steady. "Everything is fine now, my little angel."

"We almost died. You're not allowed to call me that," Ginny said with a muffled laugh, holding her mom close as tears spilled down her cheeks.

Jackson rose and walked into the hallway. Aiden knew he would be calling for a clean-up crew to dispose of the changelings' bodies and hide the whole incident from the human world. Aiden wiped his blade clean and sheathed his weapons, walking away to give Ginny and her mom some privacy.

"You okay?" Jackson asked, joining Aiden.

"Fine. You?"

Jackson nodded. "We should get back to Alliance House, it will be safe there," Jackson said addressing all of them.

Ginny and her mom rose and walked to the door, arms around each other.

"I do not want her here when they come," Jackson added quietly to Aiden.

Aiden shivered. Despite the heat, he felt chilled to the bone.

Chapter 15

Ginny didn't let go of her mother's hand until they were back in the Alliance House in the quiet of the library. Ginny raked her hands through her wind-blown hair and let out a shaky breath. They were in there for privacy, sitting on a loveseat to talk.

"Are you okay, baby?" Ginny's mom asked, pushing strands of hair off Ginny's face, strands the same dark brown as her own.

Ginny looked at her mother, whose face was creased with worry. Her mom caressed her cheek, and Ginny felt a surge of love for her mom wash over her. It helped calm her chaotic mind. *What exactly had happened at the studio? How had she killed those changelings? Had she really done it?* Her mind raced.

"I don't know how I did that, or even what I did."

"You are so much like your father. You have his heart. That's how you were able to fight them off."

"You said he was dead." Anger bubbled under the surface, and she couldn't help but glare at her mother.

Helena's face contorted with pain. "I'm sorry, baby. We were trying to keep you safe."

"How does that keep me safe?" Ginny asked, voice rising. She just couldn't fathom why her parents had concocted such a huge lie, knowing the pain it had caused

Ginny. Although knowing he was alive and had never come to see Ginny once hurt just as much, if not more. She couldn't help but feel betrayed, and it wasn't a comfortable feeling, especially associated with her mom. She felt like her parents were strangers in that moment.

"Evil things are attracted to your father. And if that isn't reason enough—your constant safety—there's also the problem that he never changes, never ages. We would have had to move constantly, and that would have been hard on all of us. Your father couldn't risk detection."

Ginny crossed her arms and frowned. "We could have moved."

"There would have been the constant exposure to demons and things a child should never have to face."

An inkling of recognition of the truth passed through Ginny's mind.

"He didn't want to leave you," Helena continued. "It was probably the hardest thing he's ever done."

Ginny looked away. "He's had other children."

"He loved you, he loved us. He risked staying with us two years longer than he should have because he couldn't bear losing you."

Ginny stood up, her back turned to her mother. "But he did leave." She took a few steps away and tapped her foot on the ground impatiently.

"He's always watched over you. It was his idea, coming here. That way the Alliance was always close."

Ginny closed her eyes against the hot tears threatening to spill out. "I would have preferred him being close."

"I miss him too," Helena said, her voice quavering.

Ginny felt a sharp pang of guilt. She had grown up without her dad, sure. But her mom had also gone without the love of her life. She had never remarried, or really even dated, even though she'd had plenty of opportunities. Ginny had always known it was because of her dad. Ginny walked back and took her mom's hand again as she sat down.

"I'm sorry mom, it must be hard to talk about him." She swallowed her own grief and looked into her mom's eyes.

"No, it does me good to remember him," Helena said with a small smile.

Ginny again struggled to remember anything about her father, but could only conjure up the feeling of being picked up and held tight, the hints of a radiant smile. "What was he like?"

"Kind, loving, just like you really. But he was so charismatic and everyone was just drawn to him. He made you feel so good. And he was smart, and well-read, and sophisticated."

Ginny smiled. "Sounds amazing."

"He was amazing," Helena nodded with a dreamy smile. "He was so generous. We met in college. He was involved in the local art scene, so I knew who he was, but he was always surrounded by girls. I never thought he'd ever notice me."

Helena laughed, and just talking about Ginny's father erased the years from Helena's face. Ginny saw her mom for the idealistic college student she must have been.

"One day, I bought lunch on the way home, and I saw him sitting next to a homeless guy, just talking and treating him like a human being. I was so moved, I gave the guy my food. I had food at home anyway. But your father ran after me and insisted on buying me lunch." She laughed and her face slightly flushed. "We ended up talking for three hours about life and our dreams. He was so easy to talk to. It didn't take much for me to fall in love.

"We'd been dating for a while when he suddenly disappeared. I was distraught and confused, certain I had done something wrong and run him off. It was a miserable two weeks. He showed up late one night, looking disheveled—well as disheveled as an angel can be. He had a box in his hands and asked to come in. You can probably guess what was in the box."

Ginny knew her mom was referring to the locket she always wore around her neck. She had worn that necklace for as long as Ginny could remember, but all she would say about it was that it was a gift from her father. Now Ginny would hear the whole story about it. She sat up a little straighter as she looked at her mom lost in thought.

"Your locket," she said quietly.

"Yes. He said that like the locket hid a picture, his heart hid a secret, but his heart was mine if I still wanted it. Of course I told him to hurry up and tell me because I was already hopelessly in love with him."

"He told you he was an angel?" Ginny asked, surprise coloring her voice.

Her mom looked down, tears in her eyes. "Yes, and what it would mean. That our time would be limited but filled with love."

"Why didn't you tell me about any of this? Why not tell me about the Alliance?" She just couldn't grasp her parents' logic.

"At first you were too young. And then I wanted you to live a normal life. Some parents force their children to join the Alliance, but I never wanted that for you. You could have gone your whole life without coming into contact with a demon. I've come close to telling you, but it was so hard. I didn't want you to feel hurt by the decisions we had to make."

"You lied to me. That hurt the most." There was a harshness in her voice she couldn't control.

Helena searched her daughter's face, one hand on Ginny's cheek, one clasping Ginny's hand tight. "Can you forgive me? Can you forgive me for being human and making big mistakes? I'm so sorry, Ginny. I really am."

A wave of bitterness washed over her, but looking into her mother's eyes full of contrition and love, Ginny pushed those dark feelings down and took a deep breath. This was her mother, whom she loved with all her heart. Yes, she had made a huge mistake, but she was human.

"Of course I forgive you, Mom. It's just a lot to take in." Ginny looked down at the ground, trying to understand all the feelings that swirled within her.

Ginny's mom brushed her bangs from Ginny's face. "My brave, strong little angel."

"I'm not the angel, my father is."

They laughed and Ginny let her mom pull her into another embrace. With those strong arms around her, Ginny could face anything.

Jackson knocked on the door and entered.

"Sorry for the interruption, but the sooner you, Helena, are out of danger, the better for all of us."

"What do you mean?" Ginny asked. Heart pounding again.

"Jacob will not give up just because he failed tonight.

Your mother is still a possible target for Jacob, so we need to remove her from the threat."

Ginny went rigid, palms sweaty as she thought of Jacob. What lengths wouldn't he go through to get to her? She didn't even know why he wanted her. A chill shivered down her spine; her mouth went dry. Her mom was still a target. They weren't safe after all.

"What do you suggest we do?" Helena asked, pursing her lips as she brushed the hair out of Ginny's face.

"A close friend of mine runs a chapter on the West Coast and has agreed to help you. I have already arranged your transportation, but we need to leave now."

"But how long will you be gone?" Ginny asked looking from Jackson to her mom.

"That is hard to say at this point in time," Jackson answered for Helena.

"What about Ginny? What about my studio?"

"Ginny will stay with us, of course, and we will keep an eye on your home. As for your place of business, you will be able to make better arrangements after the place has been cleaned and repaired. For now it is listed as under renovations."

Helena nodded grimly.

"Where will she be staying?"

"We thought it best if no one here knows. My counterpart has arranged housing for your mother near his chapter. That is all I know."

"As long as you're safe," Ginny said, facing her mom with tears in her eyes. She couldn't believe she was losing her mom right when she needed her the most. Still, she wanted her mom to be away from any danger. Her emotions were a tangled mess as she hugged her mom close.

Helena hugged Ginny back. "I'll still be able to talk to you. This is only temporary."

Ginny nodded, the tears now falling down her face as she tried to memorize the smell of her mom's perfume and the feeling of her mom's arms around her.

"Be safe, my darling." Her mom kissed her cheek.

Helena pulled away and left with Jackson. Ginny watched her go with a sinking heart. In the dark uncertainty of the library, Ginny let the tears come. Hugging her knees to her chest, she sobbed silently. Everything had changed in just a few short days, and Ginny mourned the loss of more than just her mother in the stillness of the abandoned room.

Chapter 16

Isabel lay on the bed, slick with sweat, her long, black hair plastered to her neck. She screamed, fingers clawing at the sheets while Marta glared at her, disgust written on her face.

"Push, woman," Marta said with a screech, and Isabel pushed, panting and moaning. "You almost finished."

And Isabel was. She was moments from dying, his mother. Jacob wondered if she knew it as surely as Marta knew.

The pounding began at the door. His grandfather's voice bellowed, screaming to be let in. Little did he know what was really occurring in that little attic room. He hammered on the door, demanding to be heard.

Marta paid him no notice as she urged Isabel to push. Finally, Jacob watched himself being born, watched Marta swath him in a blanket, watched Marta hand him to Isabel. Isabel smiled bitterly.

"Call him Jacob, for he will found a new land," Isabel said with the same cruel smile Jacob had inherited.

"Yes, Jacob. Jacob the Usurper he will be," Marta replied to the still figure of Isabel as Jacob began to cry. His mother was already dead, deaf to the cries of her son.

Marta crossed to the center of the room, drew out a dagger, and spilled blood onto the floor. With her own blood she drew a sigil on the floor that burned like coal. She stepped back and watched with no emotion as two demons crawled out of the mark.

"Destroy everything," she said to the disfigured creatures that squealed with greed.

Taking Jacob into her arms and removing Isabel's ring from her left hand, she opened the window wide and jumped out of view as the demons opened the door to devour his grandfather.

Jacob could hear the screams of his family for a few moments, watched as the room burned around his mother's corpse, the acrid smoke as hot and bitter as this moment. Then all went dark and vanished. Jacob woke with a start, his own hair matted to his forehead with sweat. His father was displeased. Forcing Jacob to relive his birth was his father's favorite way to punish him.

Jacob showered off the sweat and changed into fresh clothes, but the dream lingered the way the acrid scent of cigarette smoke clung to him after a night out. His weakling of a mother always returned to him again and again after he had the dream. She had barely laid eyes on him before dying and leaving him to Marta's care. Isabel hadn't been strong enough, she hadn't had the will she needed to survive. Marta had scorned her, but Isabel had proven Marta right. Jacob still hated Marta for her contempt towards Isabel, and for her unfeeling nature.

"I am unfeeling," Jacob said aloud, reminding himself that feelings were dangerous and useless. Still, Isabel appeared when he closed his eyes, pain twisting her features. Jacob shook his head and thought of Evangeline instead; of what awaited her and them both. He smiled and strode to his favorite room in the house.

A man knelt on the floor, his chains connecting to the floorboard where a few short weeks before, he had heard Evangeline's name for the first time. Jacob relished in the memory of breaking that Alliance scum, of forcing him to betray his solemn oath to heaven, surely damning him to perdition. A grin spread across his face.

"Please," the man said, voice hoarse and trembling from screaming.

"Shut up," Jacob said, his lip curling as he crossed the room. The man squirmed, holding his chained hands before his face. Jacob aimed a kick at the man's ribs, reveling in the sounds of pain it caused. The crack of bone, the choking gasps. The man arched his back involuntarily and Jacob brought his boot down hard, shattering the man's nose. The man slumped forward unconscious.

"Why you no kill him?" Marta said from behind Jacob,

Jacob hadn't even noticed her entrance, which annoyed him.

"Because it's fun to break him before I kill him."

"You are upset now. You will be more upset soon."

"No riddles, woman. What do you mean?"

"You know of what I speak," she said, crinkling her nose.

Marta, as a former angelborn, had strong powers, including the ability to read the thoughts and feelings of others. Jacob hated her for having these powers. She smiled at him like he was her prey. This creature who had raised him and been his constant companion the last ninety years. This cruel woman who saw and knew everything.

"He comes now to beg," she said with a grimace.

Sure enough, Mordecai burst into the room, round eyes darting and sweat beading off his forehead and upper lip.

"M...Master," Mordecai's hand shook as he pulled at the long, sparse hair growing in patches on his chin.

"Where is the mother?" Jacob asked, tight-lipped.

"The-the mother?" Mordecai smiled, then winced. "Well you see...."

"Where is the girl?" Jacob was beyond growing impatient, his hands clenched in fists.

"She, um, sh- she...."

Jacob backhanded Mordecai so hard he fell to the ground, holding his face.

"Please, it's not my fault," Mordecai shouted as he cowered.

"Where are the others?" Jacob crouched over Mordecai, whose hand went up to shield his face.

"Dead. All dead. I saw the bodies."

"Explain yourself." Jacob's voice filled the room.

"They were already there when I came to get the men and her mother. The Alliance scum were already there, and I saw them pull out the bodies." Mordecai spit, his face a mask of disgust. "All of them dead, and the girl and her mother nowhere to be seen, probably at the Alliance House already." Mordecai's eyes rolled in fear as he looked up at Jacob. His hand went to his neck as if to protect it from his master.

"How is that possible?" Jacob asked in a low voice.

"Perhaps we underestimated the Alliance response tonight."

"No, they would have sent only a few, if they sent anyone at all."

"Then we underestimated the girl."

"An untrained sixteen-year-old girl? Do you even hear yourself, Mordecai?"

"Forgive me, master," Mordecai squealed, holding his hands up in anticipation of being struck again.

"Get up," Jacob said, rising and looking at Mordecai, revolted with his cowardice.

Mordecai stood, and Jacob could tell Mordecai thought himself forgiven. So fast it was just a blur, Jacob grabbed Mordecai's right arm in a bruising grip and yanked him to the table covered with his tools of torture. Slamming Mordecai's hand down, Jacob reached for a hammer, holding it high in the air for Mordecai to see, clawed end down.

"You failed me."

"No, Master. No, please!"

"I need the girl. I will not accept failure."

Jacob brought the hammer down hard on Mordecai's hand. He screamed and Jacob grinned, bringing the hammer down four more times, shattering the bones in his hand.

"You will follow the boy until you see a good time to grab him," Jacob yelled above Mordecai's screams. "You will take him to the warehouse and assemble all of the changelings there to guard him."

Mordecai whimpered, nodding.

"Do you understand?"

"Yes, Master."

Jacob released Mordecai's hand, which would heal itself slowly unless Mordecai got fresh demon blood. Jacob reached into his pocket, removed a vial of brackish blood and slapped it into Mordecai's good hand.

"Heal yourself and do not fail me again."

"Yes, thank you. Thank you, Master."

Mordecai scampered from the room, still whimpering,

but happy to be alive.

"You trust him again?" Marta asked.

"I trust you will make sure he doesn't fail. Once we have the boy, you will return here to continue your work with the Book of Words."

After a long look, Marta nodded and glided out of the room. Because Marta was a former Alliance member, she had more demon blood than his changelings, since her angel blood had all transformed along with her human blood. In truth, he felt she held more demon blood than even he did. She acted like a greater demon. But as powerful as Marta was, Evangeline would be capable of so much more once she submitted to Jacob. Jacob grinned again at the thought of breaking her, of subjugating her to his will. It gave him a thrill he had hardly felt before, and he walked out of the room, whistling.

Chapter 17

Ginny woke up early, still with the disoriented feeling of waking up in a strange place. She showered and dressed in the clothes Jackson had left for her to use. From the sporty nature of the clothes, Ginny guessed they would be doing some physical training today, a great way to embarrass herself on her first day here. She took off her necklace, a birthday gift from her mother, and left it on the dresser. She didn't want to break it during training.

Ginny wished her mom was here to alleviate some of her anxiety. Her mom would know the perfect way to make Ginny feel better, but her mom was all the way on the other side of the country, hiding from Jacob. Tears came unbidden at the thought of her mother so far away, but she willed them away as she ran shaky fingers through her hair, pulling it out of her way and pinning it away from her face.

Ginny made her way downstairs, feeling lost in the too-big house, filled with dozens of rooms she didn't know. It was impossible not to feel alone wandering the rambling halls. Ginny wracked her brain, trying to remember the way to the kitchen and was relieved to find it, following the smell of bacon. Her relief, however, was short lived. She wasn't alone.

"Good morning, my name's Ari," the tall boy about her age said as he heaped a plate with bacon.

With blonde hair and a pile of bacon in his hands, Ari reminded Ginny of Pat. But that was where the similarities ended. Pat was tall, but slouched, making him look shorter and younger than he really was. Ari stood tall with a confidence that bordered on arrogance. Ari was handsome with his devilish blue eyes and grin, but unlike Pat, he knew he was handsome, and it spoiled something about him. Ginny nodded to him and got her own plate.

Next down was Aiden and a pretty, black girl.

"This is Tali," Aiden said, gesturing as Tali got a bowl of cereal.

"Hi, Tali," Ginny said brightly. Tali glared into her bowl, resolutely not responding.

Ginny swallowed hard, feeling her cheeks go red at the rebuke.

Then came two brothers who looked so much alike they could have been twins with their messy auburn hair, hazel eyes, and roguish smiles.

"Isaac," the taller one said with a nod. "And this is Isaiah."

"Nice to meet you."

Isaac and Isaiah brought their laden plates over and plopped down at either side of Ginny, startling her so much she dropped her toast.

"You can have one of mine," Isaac said, handing her a piece of toast. His eyes twinkled with mischief. They were hazel with hints of blue swimming around his pupil.

"Let me put some jam on that for you," Isaiah said, snatching the toast from her hand. His eyes had hints of green instead of blue. Perhaps now she would be able to tell them apart.

"Did you sleep well?" Isaac asked with a wink.

"I slept fine," Ginny said, sitting up straight and grabbing her toast back. She took a bite and chewed without looking at either of them. She fought to keep a smile off her face. These two were troublemakers. She could tell already.

"That's good. Tonight you may be tormented by dreams of me, you know," Isaac said, taking a bite of his food with relish.

"Why would she dream of you when I'm around?" Isaiah asked, throwing a piece of bacon at his brother. Isaac caught it in his mouth.

Aiden rolled his eyes at the brothers while Ari got up, threw his plate in the sink, and stalked out. Tali ignored all of them, still watching her cereal.

"Because she has eyes," Isaac continued.

"Aren't you both a little too old for me?" Ginny asked, looking at both of them. The brothers looked in their twenties. Handsome, but much too old for her. Besides, they were clearly joking with her now.

"You guys are gross," Aiden said, rising to put his plate in the sink. He shook his head and walked out. She watched him go with a slightly sinking feeling. She had barely had a chance to talk to him since that day in the book store. She wondered if he remembered that day like she did.

"We may be too old for you, but we're never too old to see Aiden's face turn beet red so quickly," Isaac whispered to Ginny.

"Or to see Ari walk away like he has a stick up his derriere," Isaiah said smiling.

"Your use of the word derriere proves you are too old for me."

"You just don't appreciate sophistication," Isaac said, shoveling eggs and bacon into his mouth.

"Sophistication is making two teenage boys mad for fun?" Ginny asked, eyebrow arched.

"It is when you use words like derriere."

"Besides, did you see their faces?"

"I guess it is fun," Ginny had to admit. She rewarded them with a grin.

Isaac clasped her on the shoulder. "We knew there was a reason we liked you."

"If you three are done being childish, we have our first lesson. You better hurry up," Tali said, startling them all.

"Don't worry, we'll see you at training this afternoon."

"Try not to let thoughts of us distract you too much," Isaiah said with a smile.

Ginny followed Tali down an endless corridor at a safe distance. Majestic paintings covered the walls and a thick, ornate rug muffled their footsteps. After several doors, Tali entered a room and Ginny found herself in the lessons room, which was set up like a normal classroom. There were rows of desks and a whiteboard in the front and stacks of textbooks filled the back wall. Ginny took an empty seat and was surprised when Ari walked over and set a pile of books on her desk.

"These are the books we're using now. I grabbed them for you," he said with a winning smile.

"Thanks." Ginny blushed, quickly engrossing herself in the first book she opened.

Jackson stood in front, clearly the teacher, writing on the whiteboard while they settled down. Ginny looked through the pile of books: Alliance History, Recognizing and Defeating the Enemy, The Angelic Tongue: a guide, Healing and You, The Angel: a history, Common Charms and Sigils, and The Alliance and the Law. Some of the books were large and daunting. It felt strange to hold a textbook about her father when she knew nothing about him. She put it at the bottom of the pile, crinkling her nose.

"Since we have a new student, today we will review the history of the Alliance," Jackson said, turning to the class. Ginny felt like she had a spotlight on her, but she couldn't help but feel curious as she sat up to listen. "Who can tell me about the angel? Aiden?"

As Aiden answered, Ginny took them all in, using the opportunity to study them. Ari leaned back in his seat, spinning his pencil around his thumb. Aiden sat hunched over his notebook, chin on hand and fingers drumming on his thigh. Tali sat stiffly in her seat, staring resolutely down at the paper on her desk, aggressively drawing hatch marks on the page.

"The angel is called Grace. After changelings and the first demons started attacking humans, the angel started the Alliance with his children. The Alliance consists of angelborn who fight against demonic activity to this day," Aiden answered. Well, the Alliance consisted of the angelborn and Aiden. Ginny smiled.

"What other qualities do angelborn possess?"

"Some of them are great healers, others have psychic powers," Tali said, still looking down. Ginny wondered what powers each of them had, what powers she had. She had done something when she saw her mom being choked, but she still wasn't sure what that was. What that meant. Aiden didn't have powers, but Tali and Ari did. She wondered what they were, hoping briefly that they didn't have any psychic powers. Was that why they were so confident in themselves? Would she act the same? No, she wouldn't act like Tali, she promised herself. She glanced at her again, Tali's heart-shaped face was drawn into a scowl as she doodled on her piece of paper. Ginny wondered once again why Tali seemed so angry.

"Do all descendants of the angel join the Alliance?"

"No, you have to come in contact with demon blood in order to activate your angelborn traits and become a member," Aiden answered again. But how had Aiden become a member when he wasn't even angelborn? Ginny longed to know.

"Precisely," Jackson continued. "Angel blood is so strong that even to the hundredth generation removed from the angel, when coming into contact with demon blood, it will activate. Now who can tell me about the first demon? Tali?"

"His name was Shemiazaz, and he was sent to earth to help men, but he sinned greatly."

At the mention of Shemiazaz, Ginny perked up. She recalled her dream and the image of his face as he screamed in a rage, black chains binding him, was seared into her memory. It gave her chills and she leaned forward to hear more.

"What were his sins?"

"He tried to make himself a god to the men he corrupted. He let them drink his blood in order to gain powers, he mated with human women without permission, he taught men arts they were forbidden to learn, and finally, he killed an innocent. That's when he was transformed from an angel into a demon. The heavenly fire of the soul burned him, and he was chained in the darkest pits of perdition for all eternity." Tali now seemed bored as she shifted in her seat, but Ginny felt even more curiosity. This was all eerily like her dream.

"Shemiazaz was punished for his many sins and reprehensible behavior, but why is the angel Grace not forsaken for having descendants himself?" Jackson asked, eyebrow raised.

"God gave him a mandate to father warriors to keep humans safe," Aiden said, looking up at Jackson.

"Is Shemiazaz the only demon? Ari?"

Ari shook his head. "No, he is the greatest of the greater demons. Other fallen angels are also chained in Tartarus, the deepest pits of perdition. And when changelings are killed, they become lesser demons."

"Can demons enter our realm? Tali?"

She looked up to answer this one, her hands clasped together on top of her desk. "They can be summoned through a ritual or by a portal for a certain amount of time. Even greater demons can be summoned."

"Exactly, even Shemiazaz himself can be summoned here, though he still remains in his chains, and then he remains for only a limited amount of time. He enters our realm at the detriment of the human who summons him. He uses their life-force to make himself corporeal in the mortal realm. It also feeds his powers when he is in this realm." Ginny shivered at the thought.

"And how many realms are there?"

"Four. The heavenly realm, the ephemeral realm, the mortal realm, and perdition," Ari said.

"Any questions?" Jackson said looking at Ginny, but when she shook her head, he went on. "Then let us move on to healing."

By the time lunch came, Ginny's head was swimming, trying to absorb an impossible amount of information. They had talked about healing charms, how to pronounce and write multiple words in the Angelic Tongue, which Ginny would have to learn quickly, since the Alliance used it for everything they did. It was like suddenly needing to use Latin in everyday life. Then there had been Alliance laws and rules to obey, which were tedious to go through, not to mention boring.

Learning about demons and changelings had been both fascinating and terrifying. Ginny felt exhausted and merely picked at her lunch while the others talked. Her food seemed tasteless as she shuffled it around her plate.

"You better eat up. You have us next," Isaac said, sidling up to Ginny.

"What do you teach?"

"The fun stuff," Isaiah said.

"They train us in fighting. It's the best part of the day," Ari said. "You'll love it."

"Of course she'll love it, she'll be with us," Isaiah said.

Ginny blushed, but couldn't help laughing at the way Isaiah wiggled his eyebrows at her as Ari scowled.

"I'm not one for violence. I don't think I'll be any good at fighting," Ginny said.

Tali snorted and rolled her eyes.

"I bet you'll be fine," Ari said with a reassuring smile, surprising her. "Angels are fierce warriors, you know."

"Well angel blood or not, I'm not a fierce warrior or a warrior, at all."

"You're telling me." Tali scoffed.

Aiden gave Tali a look before turning to Ginny. "You'll be fine. It'll be second-nature to you, I bet."

"Never fear. You'll be in good hands," Isaac said, holding out his.

"As long as those hands behave."

"You wound me." He clutched at his chest.

She laughed. "I might in your class."

"Now that's not easily done." He wiped his hand over his brow and lounged in his seat.

"Unless you're me," Isaiah said with a wink.

Tali stood up and addressed Aiden, "Come walk with me, I have something to talk to you about."

Aiden got up and followed her out without a word. Ginny found herself frowning, but quickly erased all emotion from her face.

"They seem close," Ginny ventured. Isaac and Isaiah exchanged looks.

"Yeah, they've always been close. Ever since Aiden came here," Isaac said diplomatically.

"That's just because she's the only one who wants to be friends with him," Ari said with a smirk. His hair was tame compared to Pat, and Ari kept it slicked back from his face where Pat's fell into his eyes at all times. She noted just how different they were. Ari's lip curled up and he slicked a strand back behind his ear, fastidious.

"That's not true, is it?" Ginny asked.

"Ginny, you really should be more careful about who you associate with here. Aiden is the lowest of the low, in every sense of the word. I mean he shouldn't even be here in the first place, except Jackson's always had a soft spot for him since he's an orphan."

Ginny was taken aback by his words but managed to

say, "Well Aiden is the one who saved me from Jacob."

Ari shook his head with a sneer. "He got lucky."

"How long has Aiden been friends with Tali?" Ginny asked, trying to change the subject.

"Well, he came here when he was ten, so seven years or so," Isaac said.

"That's a long time," Ginny said with a sinking feeling.

"Doesn't mean much though," Isaiah said, patting her shoulder.

"What do you mean?"

"Sometimes you can feel closer to someone new because they understand you better than someone who's known you for a long time."

"That's the problem with people who've known you all their life, they never let you change. You always have to be the person you were, instead of just being yourself," Isaac said, nodding.

"I never thought of it that way."

"We wax philosophical sometimes, like every third Tuesday. Now come on, it's time for class."

Training was in the giant gymnasium on the main floor of the house where they'd gotten their weapons to save her mom. The floor was covered in blue mats and little stations of weapons dotted the area. The back wall was covered in weapons ranging from a mace to huge swords that looked too heavy to pick up, all shimmering.

Training was even harder than she'd feared. They worked on strength training for the first hour, doing sprints and push-ups and lunges. Ginny had hardly caught her breath before they moved on to fighting techniques and sparring. She worked one-on-one with Isaiah who was very patient with her, but also not afraid to hit her as he taught her blocks. And then, just when Ginny thought she'd collapse, they had weapons training. Exhausted, the weight and balance of each weapon felt wrong in her hands. Ginny was clumsy and out of shape, but the brothers kept at her until the very last minute, when she did collapse on the mat.

"Way to keep going till the end," Isaac said, patting her back.

"Don't worry, you'll get stronger, and it won't be so bad," Isaiah said, stretching his arm lazily.

"Drink water and stretch if you want to walk tomorrow."

"We'll be right back at it then. No way out."

Ginny looked up at their smiling faces in disbelief. How were they not even winded when she was gasping for air? She looked around and was completely embarrassed to find that everyone but her appeared to be fine. Tali was looking at her nails while Ari and Aiden put mats away.

"And we won't have pity on you tomorrow," Isaac said, walking away.

Isaiah gave her a wave. "We don't know what pity is," he said with a shrug, then laughed.

All Ginny could do was nod as she wiped the sweat off her brow and started some light stretches. The brothers were right; she'd be feeling it tomorrow.

"Drink as much water as you can," Aiden said, handing her a bottle. "It'll help."

"Thanks." She took a long drink, gulping down the refreshing water. "I can't believe you guys train this hard every day."

"We have to. You saw how fast and strong those changelings were."

"I'll never be a good fighter."

"Once you build up your endurance, you'll be the best fighter here."

"When pigs fly."

"Ari flew to Paris just last week."

Ginny couldn't help but to burst out laughing. She glanced at Ari who was standing by the doors imperiously, nose in the air near the door. Somehow seeing him act so regal made her laugh even harder.

"You're horrible," she said, still giggling

"You're laughing," Aiden said, raising a brow.

"I'm horrible too, of course."

Ginny gorged herself at dinner, ravenous from the workout. After dinner was done, she wandered down to the garden in the spacious backyard. She sat down on a bench near a tinkling wind chime, feeling peaceful for the first time in days.

"Am I interrupting?" Aiden said from behind her.

"Not at all. It's a public space."

"How was your first real day here?" he asked, sitting

next to her, his chin in his hand.

"Exhausting and strange."

"Strange?" He looked at her thoughtfully, and she was surprised by just how blue his eyes were.

"Strange to be surrounded by people I don't know, to wake up in a new place, to have my mother hiding God knows where, not seeing Pat, not going to the studio...." Her heart began to ache as she contemplated all the things that had changed. She felt like she had lost so much, so quickly. And she felt the loss deeply as she stared off into the night. "It's a bit surreal."

"It took me a while to get used to it, too."

Ari's words came back to her, and Ginny longed to ask Aiden about how he came to the Alliance, about what had made Aiden an orphan, but knew she couldn't. Instead she asked him about something else that was weighing on her mind.

"What did you and Tali talk about?"

Aiden frowned and leaned forward again on his knees.

"Ever feel like you've known someone for forever and you don't understand them at all?"

Ginny remembered her fight with Pat and nodded. "I actually do know what that feels like."

"She said I'm not being her friend right now."

"Why would she think that?"

"I don't know. She said I've been distracted, that I'm not being myself. But it doesn't feel that way for me."

"Just because you do something she wishes you wouldn't, or vice-versa, doesn't mean you're being a bad friend."

"I thought so too, but maybe she's right."

"It's hard to be a good friend to someone who's angry all the time. I don't think I've seen her smile once."

Aiden laughed. "She's been angry a lot lately, hasn't she?"

Ginny agreed, and Aiden turned in his seat to face her in the soft light from the house.

"It's been really nice to talk to someone who isn't angry all the time for a change," Aiden said, brushing her arm. Ginny's face went warm, thankful that it was dark enough to hide how flustered she felt.

"I guess that's a compliment."

"It is."

"Thanks. You're not cranky either."

Aiden laughed, and they listened to the chimes in the wind for a few minutes in comfortable silence.

"You should get some rest. It'll be more of the same tomorrow," he said, turning to her again. Her heart felt strangely light as he smiled at her.

"Yeah, I'm exhausted," she agreed. "Good night."

"Good night."

She left him, elbows on knees and chin in his hands. He looked so small and lost, and Ginny found herself wishing she could help him. She decided then and there, if there was anything she could do for him, she would.

Chapter 18

Jacob handed Mordecai the key to the Keeper's living quarters. Jacob wished he could enter the house himself and perform this task, but like most Keepers, the old man had lived in a church, relying on the sacred ground to keep him safe. Jacob couldn't enter, but Mordecai could for a short period of time, and that would have to be enough.

"Are you sure this is safe?" Mordecai asked, wide eyes shifting from side to side.

"Move fast and you'll be fine."

"What if the Alliance shows up?"

"We have them monitored. Those scum haven't been here since they found the Keeper's body. They're too busy looking for what's missing to come back here."

Mordecai glanced at the Book of Words Jacob held in his hands with a grin. Jacob smiled back indulgently. Jacob knew even if they did discover he was the one who'd taken the Book of Words from the old Keeper, they'd never find him. He enjoyed beating those mongrels, especially where it hurt them most.

The Eternal Tomes were a series of three books given to the Alliance by the angel. The first was the Book of Words, which contained words in the Angelic tongue that could heal, erase, hide, transform, or even breathe life into inanimate objects. This last one Jacob found particularly useful, and it would serve his purposes nicely. It had brought him back to the Keeper's house to put the book to the test.

"The back lot has not been consecrated anytime this century, so bring it there and do not dawdle," Jacob said.

"Yes, master."

Jacob watched Mordecai scurry across the street and fumble at the lock. Jacob made his way to the back, climbing under the broken chain link fence to await Mordecai and the thing.

Mordecai emerged at last, dragging a bulky mound behind him, sweat dripping down his face.

"Is it intact?"

"Yes, master."

"Lay it on the ground and straighten it out. Be careful, I don't want it damaged before we begin."

Jacob watched Mordecai arrange the creature. It had a head, two arms, and two legs—like any human—but this was the golem. It was an unshaped creature made from clay and obedient only to the master that awakened it. One word was all he needed to bring this hulking beast to life, one word he had gleaned from the Book of Words, one word that breathed life into the lump of clay. A word that was now in Jacob's hands.

The golem would stand at six feet tall and hulking, with coals for eyes, and thick bluntly shaped appendages. Jacob knelt and pulled out his favorite ceremonial dagger from his belt. He sliced his index finger, letting the blackened blood well up before painting the word that would bring the golem to life on its forehead. The sigil blazed and blackened with demonic fire, leaving the word scorched into the clay. The golem shuddered, its coal eyes flaring red as it sat up.

"You obey me alone. You will guard this church without being seen," Jacob said. Then holding up a picture of Evangeline, he continued, "Kill any Alliance members that come here except her. She must be captured unharmed at all costs. Understood?"

The clay beast nodded slowly, its eyes blazed again before it stood up creakily and lumbered back into the church, taking the musty scent of dust and clay with it.

"Amazing," Mordecai said in a hushed voice. "Think of all you'll be able to do with that book." Mordecai regarded

Jacob jubilantly.

"Yes, but I won't stop at one book. All the Eternal Tomes will be mine, and then the Alliance won't be able to stop me."

Chapter 19

It was another exhausting day of training for Ginny as Isaac called them all to attention.

"Everyone gather round."

Ginny noted that she was still the only one panting, and she tried to slow her breathing as she joined the group. A fight she was losing.

"We're teaching you a new move for one-on-one fighting. This is a fail-proof way to get your opponent on the ground. Isaiah will now demonstrate."

Before Isaac was done talking, Isaiah swooped down low, placing his left foot behind Isaac's, and sweeping his other leg up to Isaac's midsection. Isaac went down with a laugh.

"Now break into pairs and practice," Isaac said, still lying on the ground.

Tali grabbed Aiden and pulled him away, so Ginny was left with Ari. He grinned, not bothered by the pairing at all. But Ginny found it hard to return his smile.

"You can try it first on me," Ari said, stepping closer to Ginny.

"Thanks." Ginny was suddenly awkward in her own body, like she wouldn't be able to command her limbs.

"First, place your foot behind mine. Keep your arms braced on the ground. Now bring your other leg up and over."

Ari led her through the moves several times until she got the hang of it. After a few tries, she did it in real time. Ari wasn't expecting it, but let out a light-hearted laugh from the ground and was a good sport about it. When it came to his turn, Ginny suspected he was holding himself back and was going easy on her, but she didn't complain. She didn't like falling. Despite being instructed on how to safely fall, she always tensed up and the falls were jarring on her neck.

"Okay," Isaac called from the center of the room. "Now that you've all mastered the move, let's have some demos up here. Boys against boys and girls against girls." Ari and Aiden walked to the center of the circle on the mat and Ginny swallowed hard. Tali hated her and would gladly use this opportunity to kill her.

"I'll go easy on you, since you're just a human," Ari said loudly, circling Aiden.

"This human is going to make you regret those words," Aiden said, mirroring Ari's stance.

"My only regret is that they let your kind into the Alliance at all."

"Take it easy, both of you," Isaiah said, watching them square off with a serious look. "This is light sparring until one of you pulls off the move. No injuries, got it?"

Ari lunged at Aiden who side-stepped and brought down a glancing blow as Ari charged past. Ari looked livid as he spun to face Aiden again. He stalked towards Aiden and then the two went blow for blow, moving like a dance. Ginny's hands gripped each other as she watched.

They didn't just exchange blows, Ari almost kicked Aiden's head off, but Aiden dodged it easily at the last moment. Finally, Ari unbalanced himself by throwing a wide punch at Aiden. Aiden ducked under the blow and with a sharp jab to Ari's solar plexus, he completed the move before Ari could catch his breath. Ginny sighed in relief.

"Well done, lads," Isaac said. "Now for the ladies. Light sparring only and no injuries. Understood?"

Ginny nodded and found herself making her way down to face Tali.

Tali sneered as Ginny made her way inside the circle. "I'm not going easy on you."

"I wouldn't expect you to," Ginny said, raising her

hands to defend herself.

Without warning, Tali swung wide at Ginny, who barely dodged it by stepping backwards. Before Ginny could react, Tali swung again, catching Ginny on the jaw. Tears sprang unbidden to Ginny's eyes.

"Light spar only. No injuries," Isaac reiterated from the side lines as Ginny held her hand to her stinging jaw.

"Then tell her to block!" Tali spat out.

Block, right. Ginny tried to heed that advice as Tali swung again. The blow glanced off Ginny's arm, leaving what was sure to be a bruise, but she was startled by Tali's strength and the fact that Tali was truly not holding anything back, swinging at her with power behind each throw. Ginny's nervousness grew, causing her arms to shake as Tali glared at her. Another punch caught Ginny in the side, taking the breath right out of her. Tali aimed two more shots at Ginny's torso. Then, with a smile, Tali took her down hard, Ginny's head bouncing sharply off the mat.

Ginny blinked back tears as she sucked air in through her teeth. She'd have a few new bruises thanks to Tali, and her neck was sore. With a groan, she sat up.

"Now, weapons training. Free time," Isaac announced as Isaiah helped Ginny to her feet. She didn't need the help to get up, but she appreciated the gesture. The brothers were quickly becoming her favorites at the house.

"Come on, weapons are the best part," Ari said, strolling over to the wall covered with short swords. "Here, try this one."

Ginny took the sword from him, expecting it to feel alien and awkward in her hand, like all the others had, but she liked the heft of it and the way it felt in her hand.

"It's a type of machete. They're my preferred weapon of choice."

"It doesn't feel too heavy," she said with an awed smile. Finally, a weapon she could work with.

"No, but it's got the power of an ax when you use a downward, hacking swing."

"Free training with your weapon of choice," Isaac announced. "Isaiah and I will be making the rounds if you need instruction."

The brothers and Ari began to teach Ginny how to wield the sword while Aiden and Tali went to work hacking away on dummies with different vicious looking weapons.

"You're not too bad with that," Ari said, watching her as they wrapped up.

"I feel like my arm is going to fall off," Ginny said, replacing the sword on the wall.

"Stretch and drink copious amounts of water." Isaiah chastised.

"I will if I don't fall asleep first."

Ginny walked over to get a bottle of water, swinging her arms.

"You just wait until we get another chance to spar," Tali threatened, coming up behind Ginny.

"What is your problem?" Ginny snapped back.

"If you can't tell it's you, then you're an even bigger idiot than I thought."

Ginny turned and stalked out of the room, her face hot with anger. There was plenty more she wanted to say to Tali, but she bit her tongue. Ginny had no idea why Tali hated her so much, but she wasn't going to stoop to Tali's level.

She stalked to her room and slammed the door shut with a groan. She didn't need to deal with this from Tali, who she didn't even know enough to warrant this kind of reaction. Tomorrow she had to face the council for the first time, and she was stressed enough about that. She walked across the room to the desk and picked up her phone, dialing.

"Mom," she said before her mom even had a chance to say hi.

"Are you okay, dear?" Her voice was filled with concern.

"I wish I was home with you. Not stuck in this stupid place with a bunch of strangers." She turned and slumped on the bed, falling back into the blankets with a huff.

"You're safer there. You know that."

"It just sucks. And tomorrow I have to face the council."

"You're the daughter of Grace, I'm sure it will be alright. They'll probably be fawning over you."

She rolled her eyes. "Mom, no one is fawning over me here."

"It's normal to feel nervous about change in your life,

but the Alliance is for people like you. You belong there."

"It doesn't feel like it." Ginny sighed and rolled over onto her stomach. She blew her bangs out of her face, stifling tears.

"Let's just see how tomorrow goes."

"Okay. How are you doing? Did you make it safe?"

"I'm fine. Samson got me settled in, and no one but him and his security knows where I am. I'm perfectly safe. Do not worry about me."

"I'm glad you're safe." She just wished her mom was with her as well, but there wasn't any helping that until Jacob was dealt with. "I won't keep you. Just wanted to hear your voice."

"Call me anytime you want, dear."

"Love you. Bye."

"Love you more."

She hung up and flopped onto her back, holding back tears again. Would tomorrow really be okay? She had no idea how this organization worked. Jackson had treated her well, but he wasn't a council leader, just the chapter head.

There was a soft knock on her door. She swiped her eyes quickly and got up to answer it. It was Aiden.

"Hi," she said, smiling.

"May I come in?"

"Of course." She stood aside to let him in.

"You've got a big day tomorrow," he said, turning to face her.

"Will it be that bad?"

"I don't know. The leaders are a bunch of jerks, but you're the daughter of Grace. They have to be nice to you, don't they?"

"Is it really that big of a deal?"

"It's a huge deal. And it only happens every hundred years or so."

Ginny sighed, looking up at the ceiling. "It makes me feel like a freak."

"Hey, you're special, but that doesn't make you a freak. If anything, they'll all be jealous of you. I don't think you realize how much more powerful you are than all of them."

"Really?"

"Yeah. I mean you were going to be powerful no

matter what, being fully half-angel. But then you had the mark. You'll blow everyone away at anything you do."

She smiled. "Thanks for making me feel better."

"I can't sit with you, but just remember I'll be there. Rooting for you."

"Thanks."

He smiled at her shyly. "Well, I'll leave you alone now. Just wanted to make sure you were okay. Bye." He walked out the door with a wave.

"Bye," she said, then closed the door. Maybe he was right and tomorrow wouldn't be so bad. She changed into pajamas and got into bed with a book, feeling more relaxed.

Chapter 20

Aiden couldn't stop himself from looking around as he tapped his foot on the ground. Ari sat with a smug smile on his face next to his mom and aunt who were fussing over him and feeding him treats in a row close to the front. The brothers sat in the back row, trying to outdo each other with their dizzyingly fast butterfly knife tricks. Jackson and Lionel were behind Ginny who sat alone, facing the raised seats of the Council.

She looked composed, back straight and head high, but she drummed her fingers on her knee. The Council leaders were making her wait on purpose.

Aiden worried a loose string on his shirt. Tali was too calm in the seat next to him, a broad smile on her face while they waited.

"What are you so happy about?"

Tali leaned back in her seat. "I can't wait to see her put in her place." She closed her eyes and grinned widely, imagining it.

Aiden frowned. "She doesn't have a place to be put in."

"Exactly. She doesn't have a place here."

"She has more right to be here than anyone else. She's the daughter of Grace."

Tali sat up and turned her glare on Aiden. "She needs

to stop being treated like she's royalty just because of who her father is. She's not better than the rest of us."

Aiden balked. "Why do you hate her so much?"

"Why don't you?" Tali's eyes narrowed as she glared at him.

Aiden was interrupted from replying to this absurd remark by the entrance of the Council leaders.

Darius led the way with an imperial nod to the room, followed by Ari's father, Gideon, who mirrored his son's simpering smile, and Ethan with his nonchalant wave. Ethan was the Council's elected member, and his biggest asset was his impartiality, though years of being stale-mated by Darius and Gideon had made him a bit apathetic.

The Council was always made up of three Alliance members. They were traditionally always from Lockewood, which had always held significance to the Alliance in the states, though no one really knew why. Two were lifetime positions and one was elected by Alliance members to serve a six-year term. Darius and Gideon ruled as emperors, advancing their own agendas, but Ethan was able to temper the two on important matters that required a unanimous vote.

Aiden's pulse raced as he watched the Council leaders be seated. Ginny held her head higher in the air, but her fists were squeezed tight at her side.

"Yes, welcome, welcome to our meeting," Darius addressed the crowd. Gideon nodded towards his family, all with matching blonde hair and self-satisfied smiles. Ethan leaned forward and regarded Ginny with uncharacteristic curiosity. "Let us begin. Please state your name for the record, miss."

Ginny stood. "Evangeline Lise Gracehurst," Ginny said, and a murmur went through the crowd. Every member knew that name.

"And you claim to be the daughter of the angel?" Darius turned a sickly sweet smile on.

She frowned. "I don't claim anything—"

"You haven't been telling others at Alliance House that your father is the angel called Grace?" He arched a brow, interrupting.

"I was told that was who my father was."

"Told by whom? Are you sure the rumor wasn't

spread by you? And done with such expedience." Gideon asked, fingers in a steeple.

"It isn't a rumor." Ginny's voice was low.

"Then you do claim to be the child of the angel?" he said, sweeping his hands open.

"Jackson thought that was true, and my mom confirmed it. She knew who he was."

"Convenient that your mother isn't here to be questioned." Gideon gave her a knowing look.

"Convenient? She was almost kidnapped." Ginny crossed her arms and scowled at the Council.

"Yes, your interesting connection with the demonspawn. Although he may be no more than a changeling."

"He's not a changeling."

"Based off what, exactly? Why make such a ridiculous assumption?"

"Aiden saw him giving changelings his demon blood. Jackson told me."

"We require more reliable evidence. There hasn't been a demonspawn in quite some time, after all."

Aiden's face went hot at Gideon's quip. This was typical behavior, but it didn't make the behavior any easier to swallow. Ginny noticeably flushed before continuing. The leaders weren't going easy on her, and it pained him to listen to this. She was clearly the child of the angel after what she had done. So why were they working so hard to discredit her? He glanced over at Tali who wore an unbearable grin.

"What is your connection with Jacob anyway?" Gideon asked with a smile.

She drew up taller and uncrossed her arms. "I don't have a connection with that psychopath."

"And yet he continues to try getting close to you. Why is that? Are you in league with him?"

"Absolutely not. He's attacking me and my family."

"Why is that?"

"How would I know? Ask him."

"We're asking you." Gideon pointed to Ginny and leaned forward.

"I don't know why he wants me." She put her hands on her hips.

"What happened that night at your mother's studio?"

She took a deep breath and closed her eyes. Her arms dropped to her sides before speaking. "There were changelings. They were trying to get my mother."

Gideon put his elbows on the table, clasping his hands below his chin as he regarded her. "How many changelings?"

"Five or six."

He raised a brow. "Then what happened?"

"Jackson and Aiden were fighting them off."

"But it wasn't only them who fought that night, was it?" Ethan said, leaning forward. He rarely spoke unless addressed, but Ginny seemed to fascinate him.

"No, I guess not."

"You killed some of the changelings, didn't you?" Ethan asked eagerly.

"Yes."

"How many did you kill?"

Ginny closed her eyes again and swallowed hard. "Three."

"But you didn't kill them with any weapon, did you? There were no wounds on the bodies of those recovered from the scene," Ethan said, looking at her with a gleam in his eyes.

She opened her eyes and regarded him. "No, I didn't use any weapons."

"How did you kill them?" His eyes were rapt on hers.

"I don't know. I saw one of them holding a knife to my mom's throat, and I just felt something inside snap."

Ethan shifted in his seat. "Will Jackson please rise and give testimony to what happened?"

Jackson stood up behind Ginny and addressed the Council. "The air turned hot and dry and a golden light emanated from Ginny. Her eyes also shone gold. The air felt full of ozone and a wind, buzzing with electricity. It passed by Aiden and me. The changelings began to scream and convulse and fell to the ground, dead."

"She can summon the Spirit," Ethan said with a laugh. "That's incredible."

"Contain yourself, Ethan," Gideon said with a scowl.

"Only two others have been able to do it." Ethan looked at her in awe.

"It is a rare gift, but there is no need to inflate the girl."

"I'm not a balloon." Ginny shot back.

"No, just full of hot air," Gideon said, rolling his eyes. "Until we can confirm your actual lineage, you cannot become a full-fledged member, but you will stay and train at the Alliance House as our welcome guest."

Ginny stared defiantly at the leaders for a moment before turning on her heel and stalking out.

"It seems we've been dismissed." Gideon joked.

Tali laughed along with the others, and it was more than Aiden could take. Anger rushed through him as he watched her. *Who was this girl seated next to him?* Gone was the girl who had always stood up for him against Gideon and his family. Here Ginny was being treated just as unfairly as he had always been, but instead of defending her, Tali was eagerly joining in. It didn't make any sense, and he didn't approve. He turned to face her in his seat.

"I can't believe you're on the same side as Ari and his dad," Aiden said in a gruff whisper to Tali before following after Ginny.

About to head to Ginny's room, he stopped and headed towards the library. Beside Jackson and Aiden, Ginny was the only other person who had appreciated the room. Sure enough he found her facing a bookcase. She turned, startled, and wiped her tears away.

"Don't tell me you're here to berate me too."

He walked up until he could see the tears shining in her eyes. "I would never berate you."

"Why are you even a part of this place? Why join these elitist jerks?" She angrily wiped away more tears.

"To get revenge, and to keep others from needing revenge."

"What do you mean?" she asked, eyes wide.

"I came to this place when I was ten. Demons attacked and killed my entire family. I was the only one who survived. When I learned what the Alliance was for, to protect humans from demons, I wanted to be a part of it. I had to do it so the deaths of my mom, my dad, and my two little sisters would mean something. I couldn't let them die in vain. Joining the Alliance gave their deaths meaning, and well, this has been my home, for better or worse, for the last seven years. I can't imagine not being Alliance."

"I'm so sorry," Ginny said, grabbing Aiden's hand in

hers.

"You were really brave tonight," Aiden said, taking a step towards her.

She laughed quietly. "Not brave enough. I would have loved to put those guys in their place," Ginny said, rolling her eyes.

"I'm starting to hate that phrase."

"Sorry. It just makes me so angry how they treat people."

"Trust me, I know."

Her face softened, "You're worth ten of them."

Aiden looked at the ground and said, "Stop joking around."

"I'm not joking. I mean, we have angel blood that lets us fight better than normal people, but you fight just as well as us without the blood. You have pure skill, and that's what makes you better than us. That even with a handicap, you still meet and surpass us. I think that's amazing."

Aiden's face burned from her praise. He couldn't speak, but squeezed her hand in response.

"I'm really sorry that happened to your family," she said in a whisper as she drew closer to him. He looked up in time to see her look down. "But I'm really glad you're here."

She squeezed his hand back before drawing away and leaving. Aiden stood perfectly still long after she had left, the warmth of her hand still burning where their skin had met.

Later, when Aiden was making his way back to his room, he heard voices below. He ducked down and peered around the corner of the stairway. Gideon was walking with Darius. He crouched, listening hard.

Gideon looked around to make sure no one was near. "That child is a problem, Darius," Gideon said in an icy tone. His head gave an impatient shake.

"She's insufferable," Darius agreed, "but she's hardly a problem now."

Gideon shook his head again. "She's headstrong. She'll be after our positions next."

"She's just a child, Gideon," Darius said with a derisive laugh.

Gideon rounded on Darius. "Children grow up. And I won't have her displacing my son. We must think of the future. The future of the Alliance as well as our children." He looked around, a scowl on his face. "Come."

They turned to walk into an empty room, closing the door. Aiden grabbed his scribe, pulling it over his head, and wrote the sigil to see and overhear them.

"She's supposed to strengthen us. What a joke. She doesn't even know our ways." Darius stopped and rubbed his face. "What do you propose we do?"

Gideon looked around him before speaking. "We have to make her a liability."

"Do you mean hurting her?"

"If she can't fight, no one will ever follow her lead. If only we can find a way to curtail all of that power. We both know her power must be dealt with."

"Violence seems a bit extreme."

Aiden's head spun. *Could this really be happening?* He couldn't be hearing this right. Ginny was in danger, and his stomach dropped with each poisonous word they exchanged. *Had the Council really become so corrupt?* He leaned forward to catch every word.

"Then we banish her from the Alliance. Let the demons take care of her."

"She's young, she could die, Gideon."

"She's the offspring of the angel, she could survive," Gideon said with a shrug.

"I agree she needs to go, but let's see how things play out first. She's already alienating herself from the others. Let's let her make enemies, that way no one cares when she's gone."

"Agreed."

"Good night, Gideon."

"Good night."

They couldn't really leave her prey to demons, could they? It was a terrible fate to imagine, especially with Aiden's experience with them. He remembered the grotesque features, the claws and jagged teeth, and the evil glint in the eyes of those monsters. And Gideon and Darius wanted to leave Ginny's fate in the hands of them. It was repulsive, and Aiden's hands balled into fists at the thought. He would make sure she was safe. Whatever it took, he wouldn't let her fall into the hands of demons or Jacob. He was determined.

Aiden didn't risk moving until long after their footsteps had turned to echoes and disappeared. His heart was in his throat. Ginny was in real danger, and it was worse than he could have ever imagined. *Could Gideon and Darius really take things so far? Who could stop them?*

Aiden immediately thought of Jackson, but paused. Jackson ran the chapter here, meaning he was in charge of the House and the kids, but he had no real power over the Council. Could he do anything to stop Gideon and Darius? Or would it just get Jackson in trouble for interfering?

Aiden crept to his room, his mind racing. He needed to find a way to keep Ginny safe, and he lay on his bed, thinking long into the night. When he finally did drift off, it was to a restless, uneasy sleep.

Chapter 21

Ginny made her way downstairs. After the chaos of the Council meeting, today was a much needed break. Ari had gone off somewhere with his parents, but the others were in the sitting room watching the brothers battle each other in a video game.

Isaac and Isaiah kept a loud and boisterous commentary on each other's moves, shoving and shouting as they played. Ginny couldn't help but laugh as she entered the scene.

"Morning," Aiden said from his perch on the sofa's arm. Tali, who was watching Aiden more than the game, sat off to the side in an armchair and glared in Ginny's direction before going back to watching Aiden.

"Who's winning?" Ginny asked.

"I am," both brothers shouted simultaneously.

"Don't listen to him," Isaac said, fending off an elbow from Isaiah. "He's a pathological liar to make up for his inherent inferiority to me."

"Don't you believe that psycho-babble. He wouldn't know the truth if it smacked him in the face."

"Like this?" Isaac asked, smacking Isaiah in the face. The game deteriorated into a wrestling match between the two best fighters in the Alliance House. They were evenly matched until Isaiah got a good grip on his brother. But

Isaac wasn't done yet, he reached his arm around his brother and started tickling Isaiah's side. Then it was only a matter of Isaac getting Isaiah in a headlock.

"Say uncle," a panting Isaac said.

"Nuncle."

"Close enough." Isaac released his brother and they both laughed as they rubbed their sore spots.

"You two are awful. Y'all almost broke the TV stand," Tali said, rolling her eyes. She leaned back in her seat and crossed her arms.

"We have to stay on our toes to teach you young'uns," Isaac said, posturing.

Isaiah sat up straight, pushing the bangs out of his eyes. "Yeah, that was a fighting demonstration for the young'uns to learn from."

"Resort to a tickle fight if you're losing?" Aiden said with a laugh.

"It's a valuable lesson," Isaiah said with a shrug. Then the brothers both retrieved their controllers and resumed playing.

"Isaac's right. You are a pathological liar, Isaiah," Ginny said.

"Who asked you?" Tali said with a sneer.

"Tali," Aiden said, admonishing her. "Ginny, have you seen the grounds yet?"

"No."

"Come on, I'll show you."

Ginny wondered if the others were going to spoil it by joining, but the brothers just gave her matching mischievous smiles. She avoided Tali's glare, not wanting Tali to mistake it for an invitation to join.

"That would be great," she said, turning towards the door, suppressing a grin.

"Why does she hate me so much? Did I do something?" Ginny asked Aiden once they were safely outside.

"She's just jealous," he said, looking up at the sky as they walked past the chimes into a hedge walkway.

"Of what exactly?" Ginny searched her brain for a reason.

"She's used to being the only girl here at Alliance House and well, you're not only a girl, but you're extra special. She doesn't know what to do about that."

"I am *not* extra special," Ginny replied, ripping a leaf from the tree next to her and tearing it into pieces.

"Your father's the angel. You're the first child of Grace in a century."

She pushed a strand of hair behind her ear. "I'm not special, my father is. It's not the same thing."

"You have powers we've only heard about in our lessons. You killed three changelings."

"You killed two. You kill them all the time, I bet," she huffed.

"Not quite like you can."

They walked out of the hedges into a rose garden. The hedges came up to Ginny's shoulder, the blooms painting the air with their sweet fragrance.

"I don't even know what I did. I probably can't even do it again if I tried." Ginny looked away, biting her lip.

"I bet you could."

"It's nothing to be jealous of," she said, hugging her arms to herself. She felt like an alien with how everyone was treating her.

"I'm a little jealous," Aiden admitted, looking down.

This took Ginny by surprise, and she uncrossed her arms with a sigh.

"It must be hard. Being the only one who's not angelborn."

"I don't let it bother me." Aiden looked up at the sky again.

"I wish I could be the same way," Ginny said with a sigh. "I guess we're both jealous of each other." Ginny smiled at Aiden, and he smiled shyly back at her. A warm, bubbly feeling uncoiled and rose out of her stomach and into her chest. "So these grounds, I'm guessing they're expansive, since everything at Alliance House is huge and vast.

"You aren't kidding. I'll just show you my favorite spots."

Aiden guided her through the gardens that faded into sleepy woods behind the sprawling house. Amongst the blooms of lilies, roses, and lilac trees, a fountain depicting a rising angel shimmered in the morning sun. It tickled a thought at the back of her mind, a memory of when she'd seen something similar before.

"It's just like the angels rising from Lake Locke," she said dreamily.

"From Lake Locke?"

"A dream I had," Ginny said, waving her hand, feeling suddenly silly. "Just a dream."

Lake Locke was on the northern end of the city, home mostly to huge houses that nestled its shores and a small scenic trail. Just an ordinary part of the city. Ginny pushed the thought from her mind.

Aiden looked up at the angel's peaceful face and Ginny joined him, searching its features for any familiarity, any part of herself. She wondered if the statue was a true likeness, and she wondered if Aiden was searching the statue for the same things she was or for something more personal to him.

"What are you thinking of?" she asked in a soft voice, touching his hand with the tips of her fingers. He turned towards her, about to reply when her phone began to ring. Pink-faced, she pulled out her phone. The caller ID said Pat. Cursing his timing under her breath, she answered.

"What is it, Pat?" Ginny walked away, scowling. She hadn't forgotten their last conversation.

"Evangeline," the voice on the other end was low and cold and she froze. Ginny would know Jacob's voice anywhere.

"What have you done to Pat?" she asked, her voice shrill and too thin.

"Oh good, you follow. Then you'll know what to do next. The old R and M warehouse on Fairfax. I'd say don't bring your friends, but frankly it doesn't matter if you do. They can't save him. Only you can do that."

The line went dead and Ginny hunched over, hugging her arms to her stomach, suddenly nauseous.

"What's wrong?" Aiden asked, rushing over to her.

"It's Jacob. He has Pat."

The ground threatened to start swaying now that she had uttered those words out loud, and she reached for Aiden's hand.

"We have to help him," she said, clinging to him.

Aiden nodded and helped her stand up straight. She had to pull herself together. Pat needed her to be strong. She had to save him somehow, and without getting caught in

Jacob's net herself.

"Let's go talk to Jackson. He can rally other members to form a rescue."

Ginny nodded and followed Aiden back to the house. She had one last glance of the angel, who now looked out fiercely as he stared into the light. She squared her shoulders, letting go of Aiden's hand. Ginny took off running for the library as soon as they entered the house. Aiden was a step behind her. She didn't let herself catch her breath until she was in front of Jackson gasping for air.

"What is wrong?" Jackson asked, standing up behind the desk.

"He's got Pat."

"Who has got whom?"

"Jacob, he's got my best friend in the whole world and you've got to help him."

"Hold on now. It is probably a trap."

"I don't care if it is," Ginny shouted, slamming her hand down on the desk.

"And that is what Jacob is relying on. We must be logical about this."

"We have to save him," Ginny said, voice rising.

"I am not suggesting we do not help him," Jackson said, closing a large book. "Just that we should not rush into a decision. I must call the Council leaders first and hear their determinations."

"But …" she began, but Jackson held his hand up to stop her.

"I will discuss this with the leaders. You will need to step outside." He gave them both a stern look.

Ginny could hardly believe Jackson's detached reaction to the situation and dreaded what the Council leaders would say regarding her friend. But they would have to help Pat, that's why they existed; to keep humans safe from demons. This was certainly under their jurisdiction. Her mind raced as she paced before the library door. Pat was family to her, and it killed her to know he was now in danger, and it was all her fault. She couldn't forgive herself if something happened to him. Waiting was torture.

"We'll get Pat back safely," Aiden said, stepping in front of her to stop her from pacing. He looked calmly into her eyes and placed his hands on her shoulders. "Everything will be okay."

Ginny nodded and collapsed into his arms, hugging him close to her. Her heart ached, but it helped to hug him closer and breathe in his scent.

Jackson came out and she opened her eyes, looking at Jackson expectantly. He looked murderous, and Ginny's heart dropped into her stomach. The Council leaders weren't going to help, and this revelation made her feel sick.

She broke away from Aiden. "They won't send anyone to help him?" Her voice squeaked out.

"I am sorry, but no. They want to try negotiations with Jacob first."

She threw her hands in the air. "That's ridiculous."

"The leaders have spoken, Ginny. I am sorry, but there is nothing else we can do for the moment." He turned his face away from her.

"Jacob will kill him," Ginny said, taking a step towards Jackson.

"It is forbidden for anyone to go," Jackson said forcefully, looking back and forth from Ginny to Aiden.

"This is how the Alliance works?" Ginny's hands fell down to her sides. Anger flashed through her, and she continued, "Letting innocent people die in the hands of a half-demon? And for what? To teach me a lesson?"

"I'm sorry, Ginny, but the matter is closed until the leaders say otherwise." Jackson crossed his arms and looked past Ginny, his jaw working.

"Screw the leaders and screw the Alliance," she shouted before running up the stairs to her room. The tears fell freely and her breaths were turning ragged.

"Ginny?" Aiden's voice was soft on the other side of her door. Wiping her face, she opened the door and pulled him into her room. The door snapped shut and again his arms engulfed her and she breathed in his calming scent. Slowly, she regained her composure, and she knew she needed a plan to help Pat.

"You're not thinking of going, are you?" Aiden asked, pulling back to see her face.

"Come with me. I need your help," she said, clutching his shirt as she searched his eyes. She did need him, but for a horrible moment she thought he would say no.

"Don't play into his hands, Ginny. It's you he wants, not Pat." Aiden brushed a strand of hair away from her face.

"The Alliance is supposed to save innocent people. It's what we do."

"We?" he asked, eyebrow raised.

"You and me."

Aiden grinned and said, "Then we need weapons. Follow me."

They walked past empty rooms until they reached Aiden's at the other end of the sprawling house. Ginny was grateful they didn't run into anyone on the way. They still had to sneak out of the house undetected.

"We can't go to the weapons room because Jackson would suspect something. Luckily, I always keep weapons in my room at all times," Aiden said, closing the door behind them. He opened his closet and Ginny spotted his tonfa as well as several knives, daggers, and short swords. He grabbed an empty weapon's belt and put it around Ginny's hips, handing her a few knives as well as a short sword similar to the machete she used, and therefore, manageable.

Then it was his turn to arm himself. He handed her an oversized zip-up hoodie to wear, which concealed the weapons under the bulky fabric. He donned one as well, and then they stole out of the room and through a side door.

They didn't dare make a sound or stand up straight until they were well down the road. The stars were beginning to peek out as twilight fell and the clouds were bruises against the darkening sky. Ginny's throat was dry.

Now that they were on their way to get Pat, Ginny felt her distress deepen into a panic as the full implications of what they were about to attempt hit her. She was about to take Jacob head-on with only Aiden to help her and barely any training under her belt. The cold hand of fear gripped her stomach and ran icy fingers down her spine. Could she really take on Jacob and his changelings? Even the houses on the street seemed to turn malignant eyes on her. Despite their lights, they were empty specters standing in the night, watching her walk to her demise.

Ginny tried to swallow past her fears and the lump in her throat and spoke just to shatter the heavy silence between them.

"What do you think will be waiting for us?"

"Well, Pat will be heavily guarded. Probably changelings, but there's no telling how many. Maybe even demons, lesser demons that is. I'd expect a large number of changelings, seeing how easily you took out the last ones."

"Easy?" Ginny's voice shook. "It wasn't easy. I still don't really know how I did it. It kind of just happened."

"Well, hopefully it happens again tonight. It's our best chance...." He let the thought trail off.

Her cheeks flushed and she clasped her hands in front of her. She had to tell him the truth since she had dragged him into this, but she didn't know what to expect once she told him. Swallowing hard, she said, "I'm not sure how to do it again."

He didn't miss a beat. "You'll know how to do it when you need to." Aiden turned and gave her a warm smile, reaching out to squeeze her shoulder. "We'll be fine. It's in your blood, remember?"

"Right," she said, squaring her shoulders. She could do this. She had to do this.

"We can't hope for an ambush. He expects you to come."

"So do we just go in screaming?"

"No, that doesn't feel right either. Just stay near me, whatever happens. Do not let him separate us."

"I'm staying close to you," she assured him as the old warehouse loomed before them. Aiden nodded, and the two of them removed their zip=ups, hiding them under a bush across the street from the building.

Aiden held his blade out and ready and Ginny drew her short sword as they jogged across the street, a soft glow emanating from the aoiveae blades. They hurried through the doors and found the front room empty, to their surprise. A long corridor branched off to untold rooms and peering down the hall, they could make out a large storage room at the end of the hall. The entire place seemed deserted, quiet as the grave. Their footsteps sounded hollowly as they moved further in. Ginny's heart had lodged itself into her throat, and she held her breath each time they passed an empty room. Soon, there was only the storeroom in front of them in the inexplicably empty warehouse. Ceiling high stacks of pallets sectioned off the room like a maze, and Ginny and Aiden paused, crouching down at the door, unsure of how to proceed.

Ginny racked her mind for a strategy that would help them, but all that was forgotten as soon as she spotted Pat slumped forward and tied to a chair at the far end of the room.

"Pat," the word escaped her lips and, without thinking, she jumped up and ran to him.

"Stay together," Aiden hissed behind her, but she had to reach Pat and his words slid in and out of her ears.

"Pat," she cried as she reached him, fumbling for a knife.

"You came for me," he said, looking up into her face. He had a nasty cut above his eye and a bruise on his jaw, but he was alive, and she was so grateful for that. He frowned, "But it's a trap. You have to get out of here."

"Are you hurt?" she asked, tackling a knot as Aiden joined them, cursing under his breath. One knot free and one more to go. Her fingers slipped in her hurry.

"Ginny?" Pat said as she wrestled with the rope.

"Almost done."

"Ginny," Aiden said more insistently. She cut the knot loose and looked up, watching in horror as changeling after changeling poured out from behind the pallets that filled the room. There were dozens of them, and Jacob stood in the doorway, smiling like the Cheshire cat. Ginny swallowed hard.

"You use this," she said, handing Pat her knife. She picked up her discarded sword and stood next to Aiden. Her hand reached out for Aiden and she gently brushed his hand with her palm, knowing it might be the last time that she touched him.

Aiden looked at her, his face serious and resolute, his dark fringe making those blue eyes even more startling. His look pierced through her and shook all the fear from her. She smiled back at him. They could do this, together.

"Now isn't this touching," Jacob drawled. "A picture perfect moment. You can save him. You know that, don't you, Evangeline? You have the power to save him if you really want to."

Anguish tore through her heart at these words. "What do you mean save him?" she asked, her voice breaking.

"You can save both of them. It's you that I want.

Come with me, and I'll let them both go unharmed."

"No!" Aiden and Pat shouted together.

"Don't be a fool, Evangeline. You can't get away from me. But you can keep all the others safe. Don't you want your friends to be safe? Don't you care?"

"Don't listen to him. He's lying," Aiden said, grabbing her arm.

Ginny looked back at Aiden and Pat, now freed, who had joined him, holding the knife in his shaking hand. Her heart broke to see them there, ready to face scores of changelings for her sake. She couldn't let them die for her.

"You won't hurt them?" Her voice quavered, and she bit her lip to stop her tears.

Jacob looked at her solemnly and raised his right hand. "I give you my word."

"No, I am not letting you do this," Aiden said, and then with a cry, he charged the nearest changeling, his sword arcing high in the air like a sliver of the moon. The changeling fell and chaos ensued as the others rushed forward to attack.

They came in groups, surrounding her, and fear bubbled up in her belly. She was woefully unprepared for this. Adrenaline flooded her, and she quieted her mind, letting her body react automatically. She swiped at them again and again, keeping the changelings far enough away so they couldn't grab her. Luckily for her, they were trying to capture her unharmed. The same couldn't be said for Aiden, who danced between changelings, his sword blocking and finding its mark as he spun and swung.

A changeling charged at her and she almost didn't have time to react. Sweat trickled down her spine and she fumbled with her sword, stabbing upward just in time. No sooner had the changeling fallen, then two more stood in his place. She slashed side to side wildly until she finally made contact. And still more and more changelings were coming. She shook her bangs out of her face and surveyed the room. Pat was still behind her, wide-eyed as the changelings circled them. Aiden was battling three at once, moving as if in a dance. Her breath hitched as she watched him, worrying that he might not make it through this as he narrowly dodged a machete swing.

A changeling jumped in front of her and almost

knocked her sword free.

"Look out," Pat cried as he threw his knife. It hit the changeling with a thud, and he fell to the side.

"Thanks," Ginny said, grabbing another knife and tossing it to Pat, so he wouldn't be unarmed. She turned and slashed at more changelings who approached her. They seemed wary of her now that a few of their brethren lay at her feet.

Ginny's eyes kept darting to Aiden, and it gave one changeling an idea. Ginny watched in growing horror as he jumped away from her and landed behind Aiden. Aiden's sword was engaged in a block, and he was unaware of the changeling behind him. Ginny screamed as the changeling thrust his machete through Aiden's torso, a red flower unfurling on his white shirt. Ginny felt her body go hot and rigid. Her heart fluttered in her chest as panic and anger filled her. *This wasn't supposed to happen. Aiden had to make it.* He turned to her, falling to his knees. His face pale and twisted in pain.

A flame started in her belly and coursed through her, at first it was so hot she thought she would burn up. Aiden slumped to sitting, his eyes glazed over as he panted, a sheen of sweat on his upper lip. It was wrong, the whole thing was so utterly wrong, and the fire intensified, climbing and spreading through her limbs.

Ginny gripped her sword and, with a scream, brought it down hard on the changeling who had stabbed Aiden. At the same time, golden flames erupted from her hands, engulfing the changeling in molten fire. Ginny bid the fire to burn even brighter and the changeling shrieked, the flames so bright only Ginny could bear to look at them. The rest all turned away. Ginny spread her arms wide and willed the flames to spread and surround every last changeling, so that even as they turned to flee, they were each consumed by the fire that burned so hotly, not even ashes remained. Their screams echoed through the room as they burned. When the last fire snuffed out, Ginny looked up to see Jacob giving her a wild look, as if he was seeing her for the first time.

"This isn't over. It's far from over. You'll be seeing me again soon," Jacob said slowly through his rage before he cut his finger on a knife and drew a sigil on the ground in blood. It flashed black and a shimmery, haze-filled light shot upwards. Jacob stepped into it and disappeared.

Ginny took a step towards where Jacob had vanished, but Aiden moaned and it brought her back to her senses.

"Hold on," she said, dropping to her knees next to him. "We'll get Jackson out here, and he'll heal you in no time."

"It's too late," Aiden said with a gasp. "It was a demon blade. No human can withstand them for very long." Aiden drew aside his shirt, exposing the gruesome wound, a bloody mess with twisting snakes of demon poison radiating outwards.

"No, no, no," Ginny whispered, trying to wipe away an endless string of tears. "I was supposed to save you." The sobs threatened to really come now. She wasn't supposed to lose Aiden. She couldn't stand even the thought of losing him.

"You saved both of us." Aiden smiled weakly at her.

How cruel it was that she had defeated the changelings, but not in enough time to save Aiden. Her angelic powers had unleashed a holy fire to burn the undeserving, but too late. Her angelic powers.... She had a sudden thought. *If she could wield fire, what other angelic powers could she have? Hadn't Jackson told her angels were also divine healers? She had angelic power running through her veins, what if her blood could heal?*

"Do you trust me?" Ginny asked Aiden.

Aiden simply nodded. He was panting now. She took the knife from the spell-bound Pat who knelt on the other side of Aiden and quickly cut a deep line in her palm. Biting down on her lip at the pain, she let the blood pool in her palm.

"What are you doing?" Pat hissed, but she ignored him.

She overturned her hand, letting the blood drip over the wound. It sizzled where the demon poison met her blood, and she knew somehow it would work. But she'd need a lot more blood. Ginny sliced another deep cut on her hand, carving an X into her palm. This time a cry escaped her. She pressed her hand down on Aiden's wound. She would have to draw out the poisoned blood and replace it with hers.

Now covered in sweat, Aiden squirmed and groaned

under her palm, but she kept her hand firmly on his wound, praying all the time that she would heal Aiden, that Aiden would once again be whole. She prayed with all her heart and through the stinging pain. Finally, Aiden gave a deep sigh of relief, and she moved her hand to reveal a small asterisk-shaped scar on his stomach where the gaping wound had been.

"How did you do that?" Pat's voice was high, and he looked like he might become hysterical any minute.

"I'll explain it all. But first, let's get out of here," she said, wiping her stinging hand on her shirt to stem the bleeding. The wounds pulsated with each heartbeat, throbbing as she sucked in air. "Are you okay?" she asked Aiden, helping him to his feet.

"I am now," he said, pulling her into his arms. "You saved me." He breathed into her hair.

Ginny felt her face go red and wondered briefly what Pat thought of this embrace. But she pushed the idea out of her head and squeezed him back, so grateful that he was fine.

"Of course I did," she managed to say before stepping away.

"Let's get out of here," Aiden said.

"Gladly," Pat said, crossing his arms. "I won't be needing that anymore," he pointed at the knife in Ginny's hand. "Will I?"

"No, let's go," Ginny said, belting her sword and the knife.

They left the warehouse and walked back into the night. Ginny could hardly believe it was the same night she had left behind to save Pat. So much seemed different now.

They sprinted back to the bushes across the street to retrieve their zip-ups. Both Aiden and Ginny had blood on their shirts, and the last thing they needed was to draw attention to themselves.

"So where should we go now?" she asked, pulling her hoodie down over her weapons belt.

"Not Alliance house, not with him," Aiden said, gesturing to Pat.

"Gee thanks," Pat said, straightening his own shirt.

"It's for your own benefit, Pat. We weren't allowed to come help you," Ginny said with a sigh.

"Weren't allowed?"

Ginny looked up and down the street. "Let's go have this conversation somewhere else."

"Lucky's is near here." Pat suggested.

They agreed that Lucky's was the best place to go to talk. Ginny found herself stroking the two tacky cuts on her hand while the boys discussed what to do next. They had stopped bleeding and begun to scab over. She thought about healing Aiden and how warm and soft, like a feather, it had felt, and how soft it would feel to be healed. She was soon shocked to discover she was stroking new, clean skin. Her wounds were gone. She was grateful; they had been painful.

They all tried to make themselves presentable as they approached the diner. Ginny scrubbed frantically at her healed hand to get the blood off. Aiden's hoody was zippered all the way up to hide the blood all over his shirt. Pat smoothed his bangs over his cut. They looked beat-up, but nothing that would draw too much attention.

Sliding into a booth in the back, they ordered, waiting for the server to leave before talking at all. Ginny couldn't help but look around for Aaron, but he was nowhere to be found. Her shoulders dropped.

"Okay, what the hell is going on? Since when can you shoot fire from your hands?" Pat squeaked.

"Just a couple of days ago."

His mouth went slack. "A couple of days and you didn't think to tell me you have super powers?"

"We've been dealing with stuff," Aiden said, glowering at Pat.

"You could have let me know what was going on," Pat said, ignoring Aiden. "I've only been your best friend since you were four."

"Like he said," Ginny said, jabbing her finger at Aiden then Pat. "We've been dealing with stuff."

"Like getting kidnapped?" Pat asked smugly.

"As a matter of fact, yes. Jacob tried to kidnap me first, then my mom, and then you."

"Oh," Pat said, deflating visibly.

Ginny rubbed her forehead and sighed. "Look, I'm sorry he came after you, but I had no idea he would. I was just trying to deal with everything that had changed and what happened with my mom."

Pat reached for her hand. "Is she okay?"

Ginny bit her lip. "She had to go into hiding. I don't even know where she is. And then there's the fact that my whole life has been a lie." Her voice was unnaturally high and Pat squeezed her hand softly.

"What do you mean by that?" Pat asked.

"Well, my dad's not dead."

"What?"

"It turns out my dad is an angel."

Pat smirked and sat back, looking at her incredulously.

"It's true, her father is the angel called Grace, and Jacob, the man who kidnapped you, is a half-demon," Aiden said, playing with his cup of water. They were interrupted by the arrival of their food.

"You're telling me angels and demons are real?" Pat asked in a whisper once the server left.

"That's why I can shoot flames from my hands, as you so aptly put it. And heal," Ginny said, showing them her palm.

"The cuts are gone," Pat said in a whisper, examining her hand in awe.

"Angelborn," Aiden said, taking a drink.

"My dad is an angel, and his kids and their kids fight to keep demons away from people. That's why I could fight those things, why I could burn them, why I can do all those things. It's in my blood." She took her hand back. "You saw what I did at the warehouse. Angel blood is powerful stuff."

"So your dad isn't…?" Pat said with a sad look.

"He isn't dead, no. I don't think angels can die."

"Well, when do you get to meet him?" Pat asked the last question in the world she wanted to think about.

"I don't know. I don't know if I ever will. He's gone thirteen years without seeing me, what's another few decades to an immortal?" Ginny shrugged and picked at her fries, her appetite gone. Her food was mostly untouched, but the boys had devoured their meals already. She swallowed past the lump in her throat and shoved her plate to the middle of the table. Aiden grabbed half her sandwich while Pat inhaled her fries. Her eyes wandered around the diner. Aaron would have been sitting in the corner with his hat pulled down if he had been there. She wondered if he would be able to make sense of everything that had been happening. If he would know what to do next. What he would say about her dad.

"You might get to see him, you know," Aiden said, wiping off his fingers. "He's visited the Alliance before. He only comes when one of his kids are there. He's just not that invested in the great- great- great- great- grandkids. I don't blame him, they're awful."

"How do you know so much about this?" Pat asked Aiden.

"I'm part of the Alliance."

"So you two are related?" Pat asked, grinning.

"No, Aiden's the only human in the Alliance," Ginny said. Pat's smile faded. "Oh, what are we going to do, Aiden? We weren't supposed to leave," Ginny said, remembering herself.

"What exactly do you mean weren't supposed to? I thought you guys were supposed to do this type of thing."

"It's all my fault," Ginny explained. "The Council leaders don't like me, so when you were in trouble they refused to let us rescue you."

"It's not your fault," Aiden said, patting her shoulder. "But we have to swear that no one talks about anything that happened tonight. Not the heavenfire, not the healing, none of this. There's no telling what will happen to Ginny if the Alliance leaders find out."

"Is she in danger?"

"Not if they don't find out."

"I won't tell anyone. Not even if they torture me." Pat crossed his heart and made the scout's salute. "They won't do that, will they?"

"If we all keep quiet, they won't even know who you are," Aiden said to Pat.

"But what if Jacob tries to get Pat again?" Ginny asked, her palms sweaty at the thought.

"I have a plan, but you won't like it," Aiden said, turning to face her.

"What is it?"

"Tali."

"Oh no, anything but that," Ginny said, shaking her head. "She hates me."

"There's a sigil that can protect Pat, but I'm not

angelborn, so it wouldn't be as effective if I do the warding. You don't know how to use sigils yet. She's our best bet for help."

"Fine," Ginny said, crossing her arms and sliding down in her seat. Aiden pulled out his phone to text Tali.

Fifteen minutes passed in stony silence until the tinkling bell on the door heralded Tali's arrival. She was scowling—even more so than normal as her eyes zeroed in on their table and saw Aiden sitting next to Ginny. Tali approached in a huff and Pat slouched away from her.

"What is going on here? Is this the friend you two weren't allowed to rescue?" Her voice was shrill, and Ginny winced.

"Sit down, Tali," Aiden whispered harshly. "Did you bring it?"

"Of course I did, I carry it everywhere," she said, waving for Pat to move over and sitting down. "Although I don't know why I should help any of you."

"He needs protection, Tali."

"No way, we were given strict instructions if you remember."

"This has nothing to do with him," Ginny ventured. "He's innocent. Just a human who needs our help. Please, Tali. It's what the Alliance does."

Tali flashed Ginny an angry look, but finally heaved a sigh.

"Fine, but only because he's a human in danger, and not to help either of you." Tali pulled her scribe necklace over her head. Tali held the scribe like chalk and turned in her seat to face Pat. "Your hand," Tali said, holding out her own for his.

Pat held his hand out nervously. Tali seemed to be praying, her lips moved silently, eyes closed. Aiden seemed to know what was happening, but Ginny watched eagerly. Finally, Tali opened her eyes and slowly wrote on Pat's hand in the glyphs that Ginny had come to associate with the Angelic Tongue. The sigil glowed bright gold once before sinking into Pat's skin and vanishing. Pat sighed deeply and marveled at his hand.

"That was cool," he said, staring from his hand to Tali.

"That will keep you safe," Tali said with a shrug.

"Thanks," Pat beamed at her, and Ginny felt strangely

uncomfortable.

"Now spill," Tali said, turning to look at Aiden and Ginny.

"Nothing to tell," Aiden said too brightly. Flagging the server down for the bill.

"I'm serious. I risked a lot to come here and help your friend," Tali said friend rather forcefully in Ginny's direction.

"And I'm grateful," Ginny rushed to say. "This had nothing to do with him. You did a great thing, helping to protect him. That's all Aiden and I were trying to do."

"But you weren't sanctioned to do anything. You might not get in trouble, princess, but how could you get Aiden in trouble?" Tali said as she glared at Ginny.

Ginny was taken aback. "What are you talking about?"

"The leaders have been waiting for a reason to kick him out since he joined, and now you've pretty much guaranteed that they can by mixing him up in your affairs. How could you be so stupid?"

Ginny was shocked. She looked at Aiden, but he was studiously examining his water, and Ginny had to wonder if Tali's words were true.

"I didn't mean...."

"You don't think about anyone but yourself. That's why." Tali glared at Ginny.

"Hey, that's not fair," Pat said, sitting up in his seat. "She didn't know about any of that, otherwise she wouldn't have brought him along, right?"

"Of course I didn't know." Ginny hissed.

"What's done is done, and is nobody's fault but my own. I can make my own decisions, Tali," Aiden said, sitting up straighter himself. "If Pat is safely warded, we better get back to the house. Tali, you should go ahead of us so they don't know you were with us."

"I'm not scared," Tali said standing.

"They cannot know about Pat," he said, looking her in the eye.

"They won't hear about him from me." She crossed her arms and headed for the door.

Pat, Ginny, and Aiden paid in silence. Outside, Ginny said an awkward goodbye to Pat, unsure when she'd be able to see him again. She wanted to give him a hug, grateful that he was okay, but he rushed off to talk to Tali unphased. Ginny felt exhausted physically and emotionally and began to walk back to the house. Aiden jogged to catch up and her stomach wrenched with guilt. Had she really gotten him kicked out of the only home he had?

"You should walk Tali back," she said with a sigh.

Aiden laughed. "She's a big girl, she can handle walking back herself."

"Please," Ginny said with urgency, watching Tali scurry to catch up. She couldn't handle any more of Tali right now. Not now that her heart was breaking with the realization she had gotten Aiden kicked out of the Alliance. With that final plea, Ginny turned and hurried away from them. The night felt unforgiving and vast as it surrounded her.

Chapter 22

Aiden watched Ginny walk away into the gloom as he waited for Tali to catch up with him, feeling strange. He definitely did not prefer Tali's company to Ginny's at the moment. He recalled how much Tali had harassed him, trying to find out what he was doing when he was tracking Jacob and prepared himself for an even worse onslaught of questions.

"You have a lot of nerve," Tali said as soon as she had reached him.

"Yep," he said, turning and walking without looking at her.

"If you think you're not going to tell me what's going on after I came all the way out here—" she began.

Aiden shook his head. "I'm really not."

Why did Tali have to be so stubborn? She never knew how to take no for an answer, especially when she wanted her way. But after almost dying and fighting all those changelings, Aiden was far from in the mood to cater to her whims. This secret was too important, and as much as he hated to admit it, he couldn't trust Tali with this. He recalled her laughter as the Council belittled Ginny and his jaw clenched.

"Yes, you are," she said, poking him.

Swatting her hand away, he resumed walking in

silence. Just like the walk to the warehouse hadn't done anything to ease his mind, this walk through these silent streets stifled him. He wanted to run, to expel this disquiet from him. But he dreaded getting to the house as much as he dreaded this feeling.

"What's gotten into you? Since when do you not trust me? I'm your best friend." Her voice sounded wounded, and Aiden heaved a sigh.

"Since you hate Ginny for no reason," Aiden said, surprising himself. "Since you smile at the fact she has to face the Council again. I'm not stupid."

"That's not fair."

"You've been anything but fair to her," Aiden said, waving his arms.

She pointed at him. "And you've been completely blinded by her. You have been since day one."

"What has she done that's so wrong?" Aiden asked, turning to face her.

"She's entitled," Tali said, turning her face up.

"She's not entitled."

Tali flushed. "She stole my best friend. You can't deny that."

Aiden looked skyward, wishing this conversation would end. His stomach twisted. "I'm not a possession. I can't be stolen. You're the one that's sullen and antagonizing and impossible to talk to."

"I'm impossible to talk to? You won't talk to anyone but her. I've been trying to talk to you, but you just leave."

"No, you get mad and walk away."

"Why shouldn't I get mad?" she asked, rounding on him. They stopped to a halt and Aiden was surprised to see Tali was trembling. She glared at him before continuing. "After all we've been through and now you don't have time for me."

"I'm just tired of arguing with you. That goes double if it's an argument about Ginny."

"She's the only thing you talk about anymore."

Aiden threw his hands in the air. "You're arguing with me about her right now."

"Yes, we're arguing. I don't have to blindly comply with everything you say," she said, putting her hands on her hips and staring at him defiantly.

"And neither do I," Aiden's voice rose louder. He rubbed his neck before continuing, "Aren't you tired of being angry? I'm tired of you being angry."

"Well I'm sorry my feelings aren't convenient to you."

"That's not what I meant." Aiden wished he could just speed up and leave Tali and this argument behind him.

"You're not my friend," Tali said, her voice cracking. Aiden's arms fell to his sides and he looked at her closely, feeling awful. Tali never cried.

"I am." He spoke quietly but firmly.

Aiden placed his hand upon her shoulder. Her wide brown eyes and unguarded expression made her look years younger. She was the little girl who beat on Ari when he picked on Aiden, the girl who faced the Council leaders and praised Aiden, the girl who had become part of his family at Alliance. Tali had been there for him, and he had always confided in her in the past. But she seemed so different now than the girl she had always been, the girl he had trusted with his life. He was saddened to know he couldn't trust her now.

"I am your friend, but whatever hatred you have for Ginny has changed you. You must realize that."

Her look pierced through him. "The only one who's changed is you."

"Maybe we both have changed," he said, nodding.

Her eyes glistened as she appraised him. "So that's it for you? Seven years of friendship means nothing to you?"

"No, you're the one issuing ultimatums. I'm not going to choose between you and her, and a real friend wouldn't make me choose between anyone." He met her gaze without wavering. He couldn't believe it had come to this. Was she really willing to write him off because of Ginny?

"Well, I guess that makes me not your friend."

"Don't do this, Tali. Please," Aiden said, looking up at the sky again through bleary eyes. He was losing his only friend at the Alliance, and he was losing the Alliance all at once. A weight sank into his chest, making him leaden.

"You did this," Tali said, anger flashing.

He looked at her, hardly believing this was happening. "You're the one insisting—"

"Good bye." Tali drew herself up and instantly all the vulnerability she had shown vanished. She looked at him fiercely. "Next time you need a favor, ask someone else." She strode away from him, her head held high.

Aiden watched her grow smaller in the darkness before he moved again. A knot had twisted itself in between his shoulders, and he felt stretched so thin he was in danger of cracking. The solitary night did nothing to assuage him. Finally, he neared Alliance House filled with foreboding. Everything Tali had said at Lucky's was true. This place he had known since childhood might not be his home much longer. Ginny stood there, waiting for him at the gate despite refusing to walk back with him.

"You okay?" She reached up to brush his bangs out of his eyes. Her touch brought a lump to his throat, so he just nodded. She smiled knowingly. "How's your stomach?"

"Perfect now, thanks to someone."

He drew his shirts up high to show her his bare skin, completely free of all injuries save his new scar. A rustle in the bushes made him self-conscious though, and he hastily pulled his shirts back down, taking care to tug his zip-up down to cover his bloodstained tee.

"I'm so glad you're okay."

"It's all thanks to you." Warmth flooded him as he watched her smile at him.

"But I still got you in trouble," Ginny said with a frown.

"You had nothing to do with it. It was my decision."

"I convinced you to go," she said looking up at him, concern marking her features.

"No, I made the choice to do what I thought was right. And I knew the consequences. You didn't do anything wrong."

"I—"

"Let's get inside," he interrupted her. As much as he didn't want to face the inevitable, he hated Ginny blaming herself more. His possible expulsion from the Alliance was enough torment to deal with. He didn't want to add Ginny's guilt to the pile of exhausting emotions Aiden already felt weighted down with.

They walked through the front doors, not bothering with stealth anymore. Jackson immediately ambushed them.

"Where on earth have you two been? Unheard of levels of demonic activity almost break the sensors, and then everything goes white static. Our crews found nothing, absolutely nothing, when they arrived. But I am sure that does not surprise the two of you. The Council leaders were outraged to hear you disobeyed their orders. There will be a full tribunal. Now tell me what has happened.”

Jackson had never looked this disheveled before. His hair stuck up in tufts from running his hands through it and his shirt was partially untucked. He looked furious, but the worst part was he looked terrified whenever his eyes met Aiden’s.

“Nothing happened,” Aiden said evenly, though his stomach was doing flips. Aiden had never kept a secret from Jackson before, and it didn’t sit well with him.

“You rescued her friend.”

“We didn’t do anything.”

“Do not lie to me, Aiden. Her friend is captured and you two disappear. They found evidence he was being held at the warehouse. They know you were involved.”

“They don’t know anything, and that’s how it’s going to stay.”

Jackson ran his hand through his hair again. “Aiden, I cannot protect you if you do this.”

Aiden looked at Jackson resolutely. “I know.”

Aiden had never seen Jackson’s endless strength and reserve collapse until now. Jackson looked at Aiden utterly defeated, and Aiden found another reason to feel guilty. Still, Aiden held Jackson’s gaze until Jackson swallowed and nodded.

“You two better get to bed, you’ll both have an early morning and a long day ahead of you.”

Aiden nodded and beelined it to his room, his heart smarting and unable to process any more emotions. As he lay in the dark, willing himself to sleep, he kept seeing Jackson’s frailty and Tali’s look of betrayal. It was enough to keep him awake for hours. But then he remembered Ginny’s soft look of concern as she brushed the hair from his eyes. The warmth of that moment returned. It seemed to thaw the knots of tension in his muscles, and at last, he was able to sleep.

Chapter 23

Ginny found herself in the kitchen alone and poured herself a cup of coffee with still shaking hands. She hadn't slept well, plagued with nightmares of her mom and Pat being taken by Jacob and of Aiden lying in a pool of his own blood. She took a swig from her cup, grateful for the silence.

"Good morning," Ari said too brightly as he entered the kitchen.

She jumped at his voice. then scowled. "I'm surprised you're allowed to talk to me."

"Why wouldn't I be?"

Ginny rolled her eyes and sighed. *How stupid could Ari be?* It was fairly obvious why she didn't want to talk to him. He was just like his dad, and that placed him high on her dislike list.

"I would have thought your father wouldn't approve." The Council far from approved of her. That much was clear.

"Oh, well you have to understand all that his job entails. He has to ensure the welfare of everyone in our chapter and keep them safe—"

"I don't have to understand anything," she interrupted him before she had to hear any excuses for Gideon's disgusting behavior and attitude. "Your father's ridiculous." She spun to face Ari, sickened by his defense of his father, knowing Aiden would have to face Gideon today.

"That's unfair," Ari said, frowning.

"Unfair is leaving an innocent person in the hands of a half-demon just to punish me. He shouldn't be an Alliance member, let alone a leader." She glared at him, realizing just how much he looked like his father. Her temper flared higher the more she looked.

"Take that back." His eyes flamed and he pursed his lips.

"It's the truth."

"You just don't understand because you're not a member," Ari said, nose in the air. He looked like a tempestuous child. Why was she even bothering to have this conversation right now? Ari was the second to last person she ever wanted to talk to.

"As long as your father is a leader, I don't want to be a member," she shot back, slamming her cup down.

"Good, because you never will be," he said, straightening, his body rigid as he stared her down.

"Grow up, Ari. Talking to you is like fighting with a first grader," Ginny said before turning on her heel and walking out. Coffee sloshed onto her hand, but she didn't slow down.

"You don't know anything," he called after her, but she kept walking, a scowl on her face.

"Good morning to you, too," Isaiah said, interrupting her angry thoughts.

"Sorry, good morning," she said with a sigh.

"Having a rough go at things I see."

She rubbed her forehead. "You could say that."

He gave her a sympathetic smile. "They definitely treat you differently. Thanks to your dad."

"So you've noticed too? Glad to know I'm not losing it," she said, finally wiping the coffee off on her jeans.

"Well, you might be," Isaac said, strolling up to them. "But you're not losing it for that reason. We've all noticed it."

"I've never been so hated by so many strangers in my whole life." Her stomach sank as she uttered the words. She couldn't understand feeling this way. How could the Council treat her so unfeelingly? She wondered if something was wrong with her that she just couldn't see. She thought of Ari's face in the kitchen and shook her head.

"We don't hate you," Isaiah said, clapping a hand on her shoulder.

Isaac nodded. "We like you, remember? Our kind of gal."

"Thanks."

"Keep your chin up. When things are at their worst, they can only get better." Isaiah gave her shoulder one last squeeze. Ginny felt tears in her eyes, but smiled at them both. Underneath the jokes, the brothers were incredibly kind. It surprised her how much they seemed to care about her and how she was doing since she was a relative stranger to them.

"Keep smiling and breaking hearts," Isaac cuffed her on the arm.

"Come get some breakfast with us."

"No, thanks," she said with a frown. "I don't want to be anywhere near Ari right now. He's such a child."

Isaac laughed. "We don't blame you."

"We're always around if you ever need us," Isaiah said with a crooked grin. Isaac nodded his head.

"Thanks."

Ginny rewarded them with a grin that they both returned before heading to the kitchen. Feeling better, she made her way out onto the veranda, which wrapped around the back of the house. She was surprised to see Jackson there, nursing a cup of coffee. Remembering how they had disobeyed Jackson to save Pat and how angry he'd been last night, Ginny wanted to slip back inside unseen. But before she could, Jackson turned his head and spotted her.

"You do not have to run away, you know," he said, taking a sip.

Unsure of what to say she found a seat across from him and took a drink from her own cup. She cleared her throat nervously. Jackson had been so mad at them yesterday and for a good reason. Though he slumped a little in his chair, his appearance was back to the tidy, meticulous look he usually favored. Her free fingers tapped on her thigh as she drank her coffee.

Jackson cleared his throat and began, "Coffee will stunt your growth, you know."

Was he trying to make a joke?

Then he continued, "I understand why you did what

you did. It is just...."

"Just that it caused so much trouble, especially for Aiden?" she answered, lowering her cup.

"Precisely. And it has hurt you as well, though you may not realize how just yet." He frowned at his coffee. He was right, she couldn't see how exactly this had hurt her unless he meant her chances to be a member. At the moment, she didn't care if she ever was a member.

She jutted her chin out defiantly. "I'm getting used to being hurt, to be honest."

"That does not mean I wish to see more happen to you." He regarded her blankly, and Ginny wondered what he was really thinking.

Meeting his eyes, she said, "I just don't understand it."

He took a sip of his coffee and sighed. "Some men are motivated by power, angelborn or not."

"Isn't there anything we can do about it?"

"Gideon and Darius hold life-long positions. Only Ethan was voted in." He stared out past the gardens. She remembered the angel fountain past the roses. What did the angel—what did her father—think of how she was being treated?

"Your system is broken," she said in a low voice. She felt anger rise up at the unfairness of the Council. How could people like Gideon and Darius remain in power after they refused to help Pat? It was ludicrous.

He nodded. "It is easy for systems to become corrupt over time."

She paused, guilt washing over her as she glanced down at her cup. "Will Aiden be okay?"

"I don't know," Jackson said, setting down his cup, "but he is a survivor."

"He won't be alone," she said, looking at him steadily.

Jackson looked at her surprised, but said, "No, he will not."

Ginny finished her coffee in silence.

Chapter 24

Jacob reappeared in the trees outside of the lake house covered in sweat. He had gotten out of the warehouse just in time. Like standing too close to an explosion, he had felt the heat from the heavenfire Ginny had wielded. Jacob wasn't used to feeling so human—clammy with sweat, heart racing, and a slight dizziness that made his stomach roil. He never wanted to be near heavenfire again.

Ginny was far more powerful then Jacob had known, but that only convinced him of how much he needed her for his plans. She had abilities only the angel was known to have. Jacob had kept Grace busy dealing with the Nephilim he had set free. His whole plan had been perfect, but still it had failed. Mordecai was right, he had underestimated the girl. Now if only he could control her.

Straightening up, he walked towards the house, refusing to show any signs of weakness. A vial of his father's blood would revitalize him.

"What happened?" Marta asked, meeting him at the door, looking concerned.

Jacob held up his hand, and Marta followed him into his bedroom where he downed a vial in one swig. Instantly he felt energized, strength surged down his limbs, and the tremors left his hands.

Marta pushed the hair out of Jacob's eyes, lip pursed.

"Now okay?"

"She unleashed heavenfire."

"No." Her voice was soft with surprise.

"Every last changeling is gone. Besides Mordecai." He spat the words out in his anger. How had she gotten the better of him? Even if he had underestimated her, she was still an untrained teenage girl. He threw the vial down.

"You were lucky to escape."

He spun to face her. "Tell me about heavenfire."

"It is holy spirit. It is divine judgment. Fire burns through all the evil in a person. If there is more evil than good, they will die."

"Humans can survive this?"

"Yes, but anyone with demon taint will die. There is more evil than good."

It angered him that humans might survive something he never could, but that was a useless detail for now. Unless he started employing more humans than changelings. He filed the thought in the back of his mind.

"She killed every last changeling in just minutes." Jacob shook his head before rubbing his temple.

"She really kill so many that fast?"

"Yes, and that's my problem. How can I use her to succeed if I can't control her?" Jacob kicked the shards of broken glass. "I need her, Marta."

"Book of Rituals," Marta said calmly.

He looked at her, annoyed at her serenity. "The second Eternal Tome?" *What was she going on about?*

"It has spell to control her. I know it. Find book, and she is yours." Jacob grinned at the thought, a thrill rushing through him. "Besides," she said with a sneer, "your father told you to get all books."

Jacob grimaced. Yes, his father sought the Eternal Tomes, looking for a way to escape his stone prison. But Jacob had a grander purpose for the books. Soon, he'd be out from under his father's hold. After all, Shemiazaz had fathered Jacob to help free him from his cage of endless night. He had used his great power to send Isabel dreams of him. He had made her promises of freedom from her family, grandeur, love, and protection. Shemiazaz had shown Isabel how to use the portal to summon him. After she had conceived, the obsidian chains that imprisoned him had pulled Shemiazaz back home. Having a child in the mortal realm meant having a servant to search the world for the tools Shemiazaz needed to be freed. He had sent Marta to collect Jacob at Jacob's birth, and she had raised him under the strict, unfeeling influence of his father. But little did his father know that those same tools were going to bring Jacob's rise to power. Then Jacob would be free of his father. Jacob was smarter than his father gave him credit for.

"What you do now?" Marta asked, searching Jacob's face.

"I need to rebuild my army."

"That take long time."

"I don't need time. I have the word of life."

Marta smiled, a rare gift.

"Then when I get the Book of Rituals, I will have the girl."

"I found clue to where next book is. It is here, in first book," Marta said, grabbing the Book of Words and opening it to a poem.

"If book one is found at the beginning," Jacob read aloud. "Then book two is found at the end. Book two holds the keys to opening doors, both to enemy and friend. Remember well where oaths were sworn and rebellion born. Beware the darkness that calls from the cleft where earth was torn.

"Speaking of father," Jacob said with a smirk. "Looks like it's time to take a pilgrimage."

Marta smiled fiercely, black eyes flashing.

Chapter 25

Ginny had expected the Council to harass her first thing, but they had left her alone all day. The same couldn't be said for Aiden, who was locked in the Assembly room with them for hours. He still hadn't reemerged from his room since. Ginny felt like she was drowning in guilt as the time stretched on and searched her mind for what she could do to help him. Finally, an idea came to her and she went to the kitchen to prepare.

As she was making sandwiches and packing up snacks, Tali walked in.

"Why are you so cheerful? You've just ruined Aiden's life."

Anger flared up, heat rising to her face, but Ginny bit back her words. She decided Tali wasn't worth the argument. She just wouldn't give her the satisfaction, hard as it was to stay silent.

"It's only a matter of time before he gets kicked out because of you."

Ginny finished the sandwiches and packed them. She threw in a few sodas and some more snacks from the cupboard and zipped up her bag. She was ready. She walked past Tali without a glance and made her way to Aiden's room. She could hear him moving around, so she knocked. There was no response so she knocked more insistently. He finally answered the door with a scowl.

"What do you want?"

"You're coming with me. We're going on an adventure," she said, smiling brightly.

"You've got to be kidding me."

"Get dressed. You've got five minutes."

"I never agreed to this."

"Four minutes."

"But...."

"Three minutes," she said, stomping her foot playfully.

"Fine, I'll get dressed if it will make you stop... whatever this is." She knew she was being silly, but she also knew that was exactly what Aiden needed.

He reemerged still with a scowl that Ginny summarily ignored. She turned and led the way out of the house.

Being out of the Alliance House seemed to help Aiden relax. After just a few minutes of walking, he stood up taller and his stride was lighter. They walked in comfortable silence, drinking in the beautiful summer day. The wind danced through rustling leaves and birds called to each other as the sun warmed their skin.

"It's good to get out of that place," Ginny said, stretching her arms out.

"So where are we going anyway?"

"First we're going to the park."

He raised a brow. "The park?"

"Yeah, you know the place with picnic tables and swings and stuff."

"I'm aware. So are we going there to swing?"

She grinned at him. "We could. Swinging is awesome."

"You're a child," Aiden said, but he laughed, giving Ginny his first smile of the day.

When they reached the park, Ginny made a show of unpacking their picnic lunch. Aiden perked up when he saw the food. Ginny was certain he hadn't eaten all day and hoped she had made enough sandwiches as she watched him grab two to start with.

They had a leisurely lunch. Ginny kept making jokes and trying to get him to laugh. He particularly enjoyed her impersonation of Ari. But they stayed away from too much talk of Alliance. Instead Ginny shared stories from her past.

Aiden relaxed and laughed along, and Ginny was overjoyed to see it.

"Thanks for lunch," Aiden said as she packed up their mess.

"You're welcome, but our fun isn't over yet."

"It isn't?"

"Nope, next stop is the carnival."

He caught her gaze. "Where we met."

"Except this time, I'm not letting anyone tackle me."

"Sounds like a good plan."

At the fair, they rode a few rides, but spent most of their time at the arcade games. Turns out, Aiden was really good at them. He won Ginny a rabbit, a blue teddy bear, and a fuzzy monkey. She struggled to carry all three of them around. Aiden refused to hold any of them so he could laugh at her when she craned her neck to see past them.

After a couple of hours, they headed home for dinner. Aiden carried the monkey and the teddy bear while Ginny hugged her rabbit close.

"Thanks for today. I know why you did this, and I really appreciate it," Aiden said slowly. "I can face all of them at the house now."

"I had a great time. It was fun just hanging out, no Alliance stuff or rescuing people. Just a good time," she said with a smile.

"Yeah." He grew quiet.

Ginny stopped to face him. "I just wanted to say, no matter what happens to you, you won't be alone. I'll be there. And you won't...." Ginny struggled to explain herself. "What I mean is that if you do get kicked out, you're coming to live with me at my house."

Aiden stopped in his tracks and faced her. "What are you talking about? You can't leave Alliance House. It's too dangerous."

"The Alliance is watching my house anyway," she said with a shrug. "Plus, you'll be there to keep me safe."

"I appreciate the offer, but I can't—"

"You can and you will. I'm not going to let you be homeless and alone. This is all my fault anyway. But you'll always have a home with me."

Aiden stared at Ginny for a long time. Finally, he grabbed her free hand with his and pulled her into a one-armed bear hug.

"Thank you," he mumbled into her hair, his voice a whisper. "You really are an angel."

Chapter 26

"Tell us what happened," Gideon said from his perch above Aiden. This was the secret tribunal to find him officially guilty of treason and expel Aiden from the Alliance. Aiden was only grateful it was closed so the others couldn't watch him be humiliated.

"There's nothing to tell," Aiden said, clearing his throat.

"Be reasonable." Darius spread his hands wide. "You don't want to leave here, do you?"

Aiden shook his head, but didn't speak. He couldn't.

"We know this deals with Ginny. Tell us, and you'll be forgiven."

"Are you willing to choose her over this Council? Surely she wouldn't be so noble, so why should you?" Gideon tamped his pen down on the podium.

"There's nothing to tell," Aiden repeated automatically.

"What about the human, Pat?" Darius asked, trying a new tactic.

"He's fine now," Aiden said with a shrug.

"Where is he?"

"No idea. He's not my friend." This at least was the truth and didn't hurt him to say.

"And yet you went to his aid. Did Ginny force you to

go?" Gideon asked, putting his pen down and flexing his fingers.

"No one forced me to do anything."

"Then you admit your own guilt."

"Will you tell us nothing of that night?" Ethan asked, chewing on his lip.

Aiden shook his head, feeling bad for Ethan who looked as pained about what was happening as Aiden felt.

"Then we know what to do," Gideon said, sitting up taller in his seat, the corner of his mouth smirking upward. Gideon had been waiting to say these words a long time. "Aiden King, you have been charged with treason against this Council and, therefore, the Alliance. You have broken the vows you swore to uphold and henceforth and forevermore you—"

Blinding gold light flashed through the room, knocking the Council leaders from their chairs. Aiden looked up and fell to his knees in awe. The angel stood before him, tall and muscled with strawberry blond curls, hair glinting alternately red and gold as he flexed his massive wings and turned to face the Council. His golden eyes burned with anger, and the Council leaders trembled as they found their seats again. Angels were first and foremost warriors, a concept that Aiden now fully understood.

The angel emanated power so that the air was filled with an electric current buzzing against Aiden's skin and the air sweltered as if Aiden was standing next to a raging fire. He had come to associate these sensations with Ginny, but this was far stronger than even she was, and Aiden was speechless against such power. The fierce countenance of the angel and the fact that he was dressed in battle gear, complete with a shimmering aoiveae blade the likes of which Aiden had never seen, was enough to make Aiden tremble as he knelt behind the angel.

The angel's eyes softened as he glanced at Aiden, or at least it seemed that way to Aiden, and the fear snapped inside his chest, allowing him to breathe fully.

"Rise, Aiden. You have not displeased me," the angel said in a clear voice that reminded Aiden of music, both of tinkling bells and deep clanging gongs. And like the summer sun, it somehow warmed him.

The angel was both exquisitely beautiful and

menacing as he faced the Council again. He stood nine or ten feet tall and seemed encased in gold, a golden sheen on his skin and on the iridescent feathers of his wings.

"Welcome, Oh Mighty One," Darius finally managed to stammer out. The Council leaders sat stiffly in their seats, and Aiden felt the wrongness of this. Aiden rose from his knees, feeling ashamed.

"Silence. I do not require the welcome of this Council to return to my own house."

"We meant no harm—" Gideon said, wiping his brow.

"No harm? Do you pretend you do not have plans to ruin my daughter? You attack my blood and try to remove those who would help her, yet you say you meant me no harm? You dare to judge this boy whose fate will be greater than any of yours?" His voice boomed out in his displeasure.

The Council leaders shook, eyes wide as they watched the angel in his anger. The room crackled with static.

"How dare you try to punish my daughter," the angel said, looming up as he pointed to the Council.

"Forgive us," Ethan cried out, falling to his knees.

"You speak of oath-breaking when that is the crime you yourselves are guilty of. You refused to help a mortal in danger from demons, and now you want to punish one who has upheld his divine mandate with heaven when you have failed to?" The angel seemed to be glowing as he was surrounded by darkness that took the form of thunderclouds, making a stark and terrifying contrast.

"Please forgive us. We only did as we thought right," Gideon said, finally dropping to his knees beside Ethan.

Darius joined them clumsily. "Forgive us, please."

"Mighty One, have mercy on us. We are your faithful servants." Gideon braced his arms in front of him, hands still clasped together.

"Yes, you are servants, but you have forgotten the meaning of the word. You have not been faithful, but you have served and have done some good. I will spare you."

Darius laughed in relief, making the angel frown.

"You have, in the past, done enough good works to spare you. But that does not mean you will not be punished."

"Exalted One, please have mercy on us," Darius cried out, his laugh cut off.

"This is mercy," the angel said before waving his

hand before the raised podium where the leaders cowered. A golden light shot from his hand, burning the Angelic tongue deep into the wood. Somehow Aiden's mind understood its meaning. It said "Remember the Alliance between divinity and man and hold your sacred charge above all others."

"Darius Lemaire and Gideon Durant, you will no longer serve on this Council. You retain your places as Alliance members, but you will no longer hold sway over Alliance matters."

"You can't mean this," Darius sat down, mouth agape.

"Please reconsider, Eldest Brother. My family has always served on the Council," Gideon said, splaying his hands.

"And look how you both have abused that power. Oh yes, I know of all your deeds and what you hold in your heart, and not just for my daughter," the angel said, his voice becoming steel as he spoke the word daughter. "You have no more power over the Council.

"As for you, Ethan Adler, you have worked to keep these two from wielding too much power. Therefore, you will remain on the Council as the elected member, but do not give in to your apathy and indifference. You will need to be strong for what is coming."

Ethan swallowed and nodded. "Thank you, Gracious One."

"Please, I beg you once more. Do not take me off the Council," Gideon said, now weeping openly.

"You have had my final judgment and have already been replaced. Now you three will leave us. I need to speak with Aiden alone."

They stumbled backwards and out of the room. Icy terror gripped Aiden and he dropped his gaze as the angel turned to face him. What could the angel possibly want with him?

"Do not be afraid, I am well pleased with you."

Aiden looked up to see the angel smiling at him. All fear burned away and unbridled joy replaced it. "I only did what I thought was right."

"You have a bravery very few people possess. And you will do many great things still."

"You can see the future?"

"Angels possess many gifts. I cannot exactly know

the future, only one can do that, but like others amongst my family, I do possess some psychic gifts.”

“Some members can as well.” The angel nodded and Aiden found the courage to say, “But you said I’ll do great things? I don’t see how, since I’m not angelborn.”

“That is precisely why only you can save us. Listen carefully, for I cannot stay here much longer. What is it that you wear about your neck?”

“My scribe?” The angel shook his head and Aiden grabbed the key that lay against his chest. “The key to my family’s treasure?”

“Yes, you wear the key and your family’s signet ring to claim it.”

“To claim what exactly? Mom said it was vitally important and I had to protect our secret, but she never got a chance to tell me what it was,” Aiden said, looking down at the ring with tears in his eyes.

“Your family’s great secret was the first secret of the very first Secret Keeper. Your forebear and the first mortal man to join the Keepers, brothers and scholars of the Alliance,” he said, placing his hand on Aiden’s shoulder. The angel smiled as he regarded him.

“What was the secret?”

“The blade, Usurper. Hidden for centuries from those who would use it for great evil.”

“A blade?” This was not what Aiden had expected. Not that he knew what he had expected.

“A special blade, tempered so that it would cut through anything in a single swing, but also tempered so that only a mortal could wield it. Insignias along its handle keep anyone with angel or demon blood from touching it. As I trusted your forebear before you, I now trust you to retrieve the blade and keep it safe before Jacob finds it. He wishes to use the blade to free his father, Shemiazaz, from the bond that holds him from this realm. Jacob must never get this sword.” The angel squeezed Aiden’s shoulder again.

“How do I find it?”

“Your ring holds the key.”

“The numbers.” Aiden asked, holding up his ring.

“Coordinates for the temple where it is kept. All you need to do is present your key and the ring, and the blade will be yours.”

He looked the angel in the eyes. "What should I do once I have it?"

"That you must decide for yourself. This mission must be kept secret from all but a couple, Jackson and Ginny must help you to succeed."

Aiden nodded and smiled, those two he trusted most.

"Jacob has unleashed the Nephilim upon mankind, and I have been fighting them without rest as they possess person after person. I have been unable to help you, and I am unable to stay now when your need is great," the angel said with a pained expression. "I must go now. Tell my daughter," a tear trickled down his face, "tell her to always trust her heart. Now, avert your eyes."

Aiden turned away with his eyes squeezed shut as a flash of heat filled the air. He opened his eyes to see the angel was gone. Trembling, he went to go find Ginny and Jackson.

"Aiden," Jackson said, stumbling down the stairs as Aiden emerged from the Assembly Room. "The angel..." he began, star-struck.

"You saw him too?"

"He said he disbarred Darius and Gideon for their sins."

"He did."

"He has installed Lionel and me in their place," Jackson said, still in awe.

"That's brilliant."

"That is not all though, is it?"

"No, he gave me a job, me and Ginny."

Jackson nodded, "We will prepare for your mission in haste, but first I must speak to Lionel. You should speak to Ginny."

"I'll find her now."

Aiden hurried to her room, filled with excitement and exhilaration. He had seen the angel and had been given an important mission only he could do. He knocked impatiently on Ginny's door. He couldn't wait to tell her.

"What happened? Did they expel you? Hurry up and tell me," she said in a rush as she pulled him into her room. Aiden had forgotten all about being expelled.

"I'm not," he said, breaking into a huge grin. "The angel came and stopped them. Gideon and Darius are off the

Council, and he gave you and me a secret mission.”

“You met my father?”

Her voice made his grin falter. “Didn’t you see him? Jackson did.”

“Anyone else my father spoke to besides me?” Her rising voice made him realize he’d said the wrong thing again.

“No. He had to talk to us, official business, but he didn’t have any time. He’s fighting the Nephilim.”

“Nephilim?”

“The sons of the fallen angels and women. They were killed off in the flood, but dozens of them became demonic spirits who possess humans. Jacob unleashed them all and the angel is fighting them off as they possess person after person.”

“Well he had time to talk to you and Jackson. He couldn’t even spare a minute to see me.” Her eyes grew a deep, somber brown and her lower lip quivered.

“He gave me a message for you,” Aiden said quickly.

“Why not tell me himself?”

“He didn’t have the time.”

“He even talked to Jackson,” she said, hugging herself.

“He had to, official business.”

“Well what was the message?”

“Always follow your heart.”

“Great, well that’s a nice and cryptic platitude. It’s just like my stupid dreams.” She ran her hand over her face. “What did he look like anyway?” she asked, peeking out above her hand.

“Ten feet tall, red-gold hair, golden eyes exactly like yours. He was really beautiful, but also really terrifying.”

“I wish I had seen him.” She took a few steps back and slumped down on her bed.

“I’m sure you will,” he said, placing a hand on her shoulder.

“So what’s the secret mission?”

“We need to recover my family’s treasure,” he said with a sly grin.

“Treasure? Were your family pirates?”

“No, it’s this wicked, awesome sword that only a human can wield. It can cut through anything, so Jacob wants it to free his dad. We have to get it first.”

"Why does your family own it?"

"My forebear was the first Secret Keeper the Alliance had. My whole family were Keepers up until a few generations ago. Demons attacked the family and my great-grandmother left that life behind. Well, that and her father had been expelled from his Keeper position as Ari loves to remind me."

"What are the Keepers?"

"They're the mortal allies of the Alliance, they are the scholars and the keepers of all the Alliance's secrets."

"Well what are you waiting for, let's go," she said, standing up.

"We need to talk to Jackson first, the sword isn't even in this country."

"That's a relief. That Jackson is going to help us."

Aiden nodded and they headed down the stairs to find Jackson, but Ari stood at the foot of the stairs, blocking them.

"And just where do you think you're going, traitor?" Ari's eyes flashed and he clenched his fists.

"Your father's the traitor, not me."

"You cost my dad his Council seat."

"He lost it on his own," Aiden said with a shrug and a half smile.

Ari leaned forward. "Our family has sat on the Council for generations." He narrowed his eyes.

"And now your dad's been expelled." Aiden spread his hands wide. "We finally have something in common."

"Get out of the way, Ari. We have more important things to do," Ginny said in a huff. They came to a stop in front of Ari.

"I'll have your head for this, Aiden." Ari glared at them.

"Oh shut up," Ginny said, pushing Ari out of the way. "Your father got what he deserved for trying to kick out Aiden. His plan backfired, so deal with it."

"My father warned me about you. I didn't want to believe it, but maybe he's right," Ari called after them.

"Go tell someone who cares," Ginny said over her shoulder as she opened the library door. Aiden followed her, grinning widely.

Chapter 27

Jackson sat behind his desk and smiled when he saw them enter.

"Come in, come in. Aiden, lock the door behind you." Jackson cleaned off his glasses as he waited. "Now, tell me what the angel said."

Ginny felt a pang of jealousy like a knife shard inside her, but shook her head to listen. Aiden explained about the need to get the sword. He mentioned Shemiazaz was Jacob's father.

"Are you sure? Are you sure it was Shemiazaz?" Jackson asked.

"This is bad, isn't it?" Ginny asked, sitting up. She felt a chill across her skin.

"Yes, this is grave indeed. He must not be freed. At any cost."

"We'll get the sword first. I have the coordinates right here," Aiden said, holding out a gold ring on his necklace. He wrote them on a piece of paper for Jackson.

"Hmmm," Jackson said, typing the coordinates into the computer. "Bethlehem. We have a chapter there, of course. Very well, but we have one thing to do before you depart. The angel told us to search the residence of the slain Secret Keeper again."

"A Keeper died?" Ginny asked, looking up.

"Shortly before you were marked. He was a Secret Keeper, one of the leaders of the Keepers. He held all knowledge of the Alliance. We think he was tortured for information."

"What information?"

"I believe Jacob was trying to find you, but if the Keeper told him any other secrets, we can only guess what they were."

"Jacob killed him to find me?" she asked, hugging her arms to her stomach. She suddenly felt hot and queasy. Had someone died because of her? Her mind repelled the thought.

"It is a theory." Jackson waved his hand flustered.

"It's not your fault," Aiden said in a low voice, but guilt bubbled up in her chest and she had to look away. "Didn't we search the Keeper's house already?" Aiden asked.

"Ari and the brothers went, but they could have easily overlooked something of import for your mission. I will take care of travel accommodations for the two of you. Get some rest in the meantime. Tomorrow, we go to the Keeper's residence."

Ginny and Aiden left the library in silence. The death of the Keeper weighed heavily on Ginny's conscience. If it weren't for her, he might still be alive. She was exhausted. So much had happened today, the stress of it all stretching time out thin before her.

She was startled by the sudden arrival of the brothers.

"Hey, you two, follow us."

They led them to a darkened room off the hall and pulled Ginny and Aiden in, closing the door behind them. Isaac flipped on the light and Isaiah pulled a shoe box out from behind his back.

"We heard you're going on a little trip."

"Wait, how do you know that?"

"We have our methods."

"Don't worry, we won't tell."

"We just wanted to help you," Isaiah said, shoving the box at Ginny. She lifted the lid and recognized two scribes like the ones she had seen the other members use. There were also what looked like two gleaming silver cuff bracelets with Angelic sigils on them and two silver rings with a round black stone in the center.

"New scribes and new sensors make sense, but what are the rings for?" Aiden asked, leaning over to look in the box.

"Not just any old scribes and sensors," Isaac said with a crooked grin.

Isaiah picked one up. "The scribes have protection charms built in for added safety at all times."

"And the demon sensors are so sensitive they can actually tell you what demons you're dealing with."

"Blue for changeling."

"Green for lesser demons."

"Red for greater demons."

"And Jacob. He's been showing up red."

"What are the rings for?" Ginny asked, holding one up in the light.

"Communication. As long as you are both wearing one, you can talk to each other at any distance," Isaac said with a grin.

"It's our own invention. Listening charms plus a transmitting voice charm we figured out. The stone moves. Just spin the stone clockwise to activate talk, the other ring instantly allows the other to hear. Spin the stone back the other way when you're done."

"This is amazing," Ginny said before tackling the brothers in a hug.

"You two just stay safe," Isaac said, ruffling her hair.

Isaiah blushed and clapped her arm. "And if you need anything, let us know."

The brothers left Ginny and Aiden in awed silence as they looked over their new gifts.

"So this is a sensor," she said, picking it up. It was a little bigger than a watch and reminded her of the seventies in its retro styling. A sigil appeared white against the metal in the center, marked in the Angelic tongue. She guessed it would change color when demonspawn were near.

"And your first scribe," Aiden said, placing it over her neck. He had already replaced his. "I can't believe the brothers made these."

"They must be geniuses. These rings alone are amazing," she said, placing her ring on her finger.

"We should test them out," he said with an eager grin. "You go to your room, and I'll go to mine."

She nodded. "Sure."

They headed to their rooms and Ginny closed her door, feeling a flutter of excitement in her chest. She turned the stone clockwise and spoke, "Testing, testing. This is Ginny, over."

Aiden's voice filled her ear. "Coming in loud and clear, over."

She grinned. "Looks like it works perfectly."

"Looks like it."

"Okay, it's time for bed. Get some sleep, over and out."

"Sweet dreams, Ginny."

She spun the ring back the other way and got ready for bed. She couldn't help thinking about their mission with both excitement and fear. Jacob was out there, looking for the same thing, and they could run into him at any point. But she was also starting to believe in herself and her abilities. She didn't know how to control them yet, but she had survived and conquered dangerous situations, and she wasn't about to give into her fear of Jacob.

"Always follow my heart," she said to the darkness. "I think I understand what you meant now," she whispered before falling asleep.

The next day they drove to the Keeper's house and Ginny leaned forward in her seat to get a better look of where they were headed. The Keeper's house was on the other side of town and definitely less resplendent than the Alliance House, if the neighborhood gave any clues.

"I want both of you to remain vigilant at all times. The house should be safe, but we must always be prepared for anything," Jackson said, slowing down.

"Aye, aye, captain," Aiden quipped.

"Ha, ha," Jackson said as he pulled to a stop in front of a dilapidated church.

"He lived in a church?" Ginny asked, unbuckling

herself. The church was slumped on a dirt lot surrounded by an old chain link fence. Paint chipped, peeling off the siding, and the screen door hung off its hinge. It looked long abandoned and Ginny's mouth went dry at the thought of entering the dead man's house.

"Keepers often live on hallowed ground. Being mortal, it keeps them safe from demons," Jackson said, stepping out of the car. They piled out after him.

"Except it didn't work," Aiden said with a pointed look.

"Jacob employed some human men to take the Keeper," Jackson said, pulling out a set of old keys.

"Evil and resourceful. A killer combination," Aiden said.

Ginny rolled her eyes and took a look around her. Even the grass in this neighborhood was in a sorry state, tangled in clumps and full of bald patches. She felt unnerved and tried to relax her shoulders.

"Vigilance," Jackson reminded them with a stern look. They crossed the empty street and Jackson let them in. They entered in solemn silence. Already a fine layer of dust covered everything. The room they entered was the chapel, peopled with well-worn wooden pews. A small pulpit with a faded cross painted on it was at its head. Beyond lay a storage area, piled high with a mound of bricks and stone and stacks of wood.

"Up here are the living quarters," Jackson said, beckoning to the set of stairs that led to the second floor.

The quarters were cramped, but cozy. It definitely felt like somebody's home and made Ginny feel as if she were intruding. A chill climbed up her spine. Outside a car backfired, and she jumped backwards into Aiden.

"Easy there." His hands were warm and strong around her arms, and she flushed.

"Sorry," she mumbled, standing straight again. He let go of her.

Jackson headed for the Keeper's desk as Aiden rifled through the closet. Ginny looked around, unsure of what they were looking for and why her father had directed them here. She wandered over to the bookcase which was chock full of books. A few pictures dotted the shelves, and she felt guilty for looking at them. Were these people mourning the loss of the Keeper who had died because of her? Tears sprang to her eyes at the thought, and she shook her head impatiently. This was not the time for tears.

A thud sounded downstairs, and this time, they all jumped. Aiden and Jackson both drew their weapons as another loud thud echoed through the house.

"It is coming from the chapel," Jackson said, widening his stance.

"Must be the pews," Aiden said, mirroring Jackson. "But what's moving them?"

Ginny pictured the downstairs and remembered seeing the storage room piled with bricks. That wasn't a car backfiring, it was the crash of bricks falling all at once. *Had someone been hiding there? Impossible.*

Ginny drew her sword as they all faced the doorway waiting. There was a loud groan, the scraping sound of pews being pushed aside, and Ginny's heart hammered in her chest. Whoever was coming, they had to be strong.

Thud. The stairs creaked as an enormous shadow lumbered closer. With every immensely heavy step, Ginny watched in horror as a creature made of rock and clay approached. This was impossible. Its head came into view with two eyes made of burning coal and a gaping mouth. It saw them and raised its roughly hewn arms and let out an unearthly moan. On its forehead, burned into the stone, was a sigil that looked vaguely familiar to Ginny.

"My God," Jackson said as the creature resumed its climb.

"What is it?" Aiden asked, voice high.

They both moved to stand in front of Ginny, shielding her instinctively.

"I believe it is a golem," Jackson answered, and it all clicked in Ginny's head. That sigil was the word of life that brought the creature to life. To destroy it one had to destroy the glyph on the far right, changing the word to death. That's how they could defeat the golem.

"I know how to stop it," Ginny said, and then explained her plan.

"That is a common legend for dealing with a golem, but there has not been a golem in centuries. I am not sure how accurate that legend is," Jackson said in a rush. The golem was almost on them.

Aiden looked from Ginny to the golem. "It's worth a try."

Jackson nodded. "I will distract it, and you go for the glyph, Aiden."

There was no room for any more discussion as the creature reached the door and slammed his fists down where seconds before Jackson had stood. Ginny ran to the side as Aiden launched himself at the wall behind the creature.

"Over here," Jackson yelled, waving his arms. His sword glinted in the light.

The golem roared and lunged for Jackson, who only just jumped out of the way. He rolled as the golem brought its fists down again and again, losing his sword in the process. The floor creaked, protesting the weight of the golem and its fists.

Aiden rushed the golem, stepping on its squat leg as he jumped high, bringing his sword down on the sigil. But his blade rebounded off its stone head and flew out of Aiden's hand with a clatter. The golem flung Aiden backwards, and he crashed into the bookcase.

Ginny ran to Aiden's side, but the movement caught the golem's attention. It stooped to peer at her, and she held her short sword up, trembling.

"Ginny, quick. Make a run for it," Jackson said, sword recovered.

"It won't hurt me," she said with a shaky voice. "Jacob made this golem."

"Is that supposed to make us feel better?" Aiden said, standing up. He armed himself with a dagger from his weapons belt and it gave Ginny an idea. But before she could say anything, Jackson attacked the golem anew. It turned and lumbered after Jackson who was forced back into the stairwell. The golem brought its fists down hard and the floor underneath Jackson shattered. Jackson fell, just catching a grip on the planks, so that he was dangling in the air, barely hanging on.

With a cry, Aiden rushed towards the golem, bringing his dagger down on the golem's back. It glanced right off, but it got the golem's attention. It swung its arms around and Aiden just barely jumped out of the way in time.

"Here," Ginny yelled and tossed her sword to Aiden. He let go of the dagger and caught the hilt in time to block a hit from the golem. Jackson still hung from the floor, his face red and sweating from the exertion, but there was nothing for him to grab a hold of to pull himself up.

Ginny grabbed a knife from her belt. It was time to test her theory before Aiden got hurt and Jackson fell.

"Aiden, bring him to me." Ginny steeled herself as Aiden looked at her confused.

"Are you deranged?" He ducked as the golem took a swipe at him.

"No. If Jacob made him, he won't hurt me. Jacob wants me alive, and I think I know how to kill it."

"But the blades aren't working."

"I know."

"You better know what you're doing," he said in a huff.

"Just go help Jackson before he falls."

Aiden darted towards her, the golem thundering after him. It stopped before Ginny and stretched its arm towards her. She stifled a scream as it closed its hand around her waist and lifted her into the air. The knife in her hand shook as it brought her closer to its face, if you could call a boulder a face. On closer inspection, the sigil burnished into his forehead was a dark red that looked like dried blood. She had noticed that Jacob liked to draw his sigils in his own blood, and this confirmed her plan. Her knife would have no effect on the sigil, but her blood would. She cut a line on her palm, sucking in air through her teeth and pushing through the pain, she concentrated on destroying the glyph. She reached out and wiped her blood on the far right letter.

The golem's coal eyes flashed gold, and then it began to shudder violently. Ginny fell backwards and landed on the floor, the air knocked out of her. The golem fell to pieces and then dissolved into a huge pile of salt.

Aiden and the rescued Jackson rushed to Ginny's side.

"Are you okay?" Aiden asked, brushing the hair from her face. Ginny blushed and sat up shakily.

"I'm fine."

"Allow me to heal your hand for you," Jackson said, helping her sit up.

She held out her hand to him and he pulled out his scribe. She was bruised, but she was fine. She knew she had gotten off easy with the golem.

"That was quick thinking," Jackson said as he traced the healing sigil onto her palm.

"I've read about golems before," she said with a shrug. "And Jacob always writes his sigils in his blood."

"And so you knew to use yours?" Jackson asked, watching her cut fade. Ginny nodded, feeling wonderful as she was fully healed.

"Well I am not sure that would work for anyone besides you. You have extremely concentrated angel blood."

"I didn't think of that."

"Are you okay now?"

"Yeah, much better. Thanks." She smiled at him, and he let out a sigh of relief.

"Good. I want you and Aiden to go back to the car and wait there. I do not want any more surprises."

"But—" Aiden began.

"No arguments, go now."

His look was stern and she knew better than to argue. Ginny stood and the two of them made their way reluctantly back to the car.

"Are you really okay?" Aiden asked once they were both seated in the car.

"Really, really okay. What about you? You got beat up worse than me."

"I did not get beat up."

"You got beat down?"

Aiden wrinkled his nose. "You're the worst."

Ginny stuck her tongue out at him and they both laughed.

"I'm fine by the way. I've had worse bruises."

"Can't you just get healed?"

"I don't mind the pain," he said, leaning back in his seat. "It teaches me to fight better and faster the next time." They sat in silence for a while until Aiden broke it. "Are you ready?"

"Ready to fly halfway across the world and find a way to stay hidden from Jacob?" Ginny enumerated. She swallowed and thought hard about what lay ahead of them. Her stomach sank, but she remembered her dad's words and her resolve from the night before. "Yeah," she said, looking Aiden square in the eyes. "I'm ready."

Upstairs Jackson—seated at the Keeper's desk—shook.

He had found a packet of letters written by the Keeper himself, shortly before he died. Jackson could hardly believe what he was reading.

The following accounts, I leave behind in the hopes that it will aid the Alliance in its fight against the one who is coming for all of us. I cannot hide from him anymore. I am the Keeper of Secrets, and I must now divulge the greatest one I have kept. He comes to find me and to possess the Eternal Tomes.

Forgive me my sins in keeping secret the birth of the monster Jacob. I now know his father is one of the greater demons, I fear which one exactly. Had the Alliance known of Isabel King's pregnancy when her father Abraham was expelled from the Keepers, then perhaps they could have done something to stop Jacob and his mother. She aligned with a demon to rebel against the life her father gave her. Abraham was ignorant of his daughter's deeds. Only little Mirabel saw her sister and her growing belly, too young to know what it meant. Mirabel's account to my predecessor led me to believe the demon child had died with his mother, and I had hoped it was true until it was too late. Now the bastard comes for me. He means to end the Alliance.

He seeks the Eternal Tomes. I have told my brothers to go into hiding, but received no answer from them or the Alliance leaders who think me a paranoid, old fool. I know I must resist giving into Jacob, but I fear for my soul.

May God have mercy on us all.

Jacob was a King, just like Aiden. Jackson knew he couldn't tell Aiden this truth. It would destroy him. He schooled his face into a mask. He would keep the Keeper's secret.

About the Author

JK Allen wrote her first story just as soon as she learned how to write and hasn't looked back since. Common writing themes that can be found in her work address identity, everyday magic, and the type of strength and courage that can be found in ordinary people. Her reading tastes are as varied as the genres she enjoys writing, from Jane Austen to Diana Wynne Jones. When she's not writing, you can find her painting, drawing, or lost in the pages of a book. Or on Tik Tok.

Ginny's story continues in...

Heavenfire

A divine sword, magic tomes, and uncontrolled power. Can 16-year-old Ginny Gracehurst keep them from an obsessed half-demon?

After retrieving the only thing that could set Jacob's demon father free, half-angel Ginny has a new mission. She and Aiden are charged with collecting the Eternal Tomes, which teach how to use sigils in the Angelic Tongue.

They are in a race against Jacob and his minions, who can travel anywhere in a matter of seconds. Allowing demonkind to learn those sigils would spell disaster for them all. In order to get what he wants, Jacob needs one more thing besides the Tomes—Ginny herself.

www.ingramcontent.com/pod-product-compliance
Lightning Source LLC
Chambersburg PA
CBHW020820190726
48285CB00006B/2347